+
G833ℓ

·The Leveller·

·The Leveller·

Jacqueline Dembar Greene

WALKER AND COMPANY   NEW YORK

I wish to express my deep gratitude to Bruce Cronin, Shirley Newman, librarians Hilda Starbird and Jackie Tidman, Mrs. Collier's fourth graders, and the children of Westborough. All gave unselfishly of their time and expertise so that Tom Cook might live again through these pages.

First published in the United States of America in 1984 by the Walker Publishing Company, Inc.

Published simultaneously in Canada by John Wiley & Sons Canada, Limited, Rexdale, Ontario.

ISBN: 0-8027-6521-1

Library of Congress Catalog Card Number: 83-40393

Printed in the United States of America

10 9 8 7 6 5 4 3 2 1

This book is affectionately dedicated to
George, Rachel, Mal, Matthew and Kenny,
my staunchest supporters

Contents

It was a superstitious age
When first he saw the light,
And boldly did his spirit gauge
Its narrow rule of right.

And because he would not travel
In the regulation way,
He was thought a son of Belial,
And beneath Satanic sway.

He saw no more than we can see,
Nor felt he more the fact
That justice means equality, —
He only dared to act.

Author's Note

This anonymous poem was found in historical accounts of Westborough, Massachusetts, and shows how the townspeople felt about the notorious Tom Cook many years after his death. It was read during ceremonies on Parkman Day, once an annual event honoring the town's first minister, Reverend Ebenezer Parkman, who served the town for fifty years.

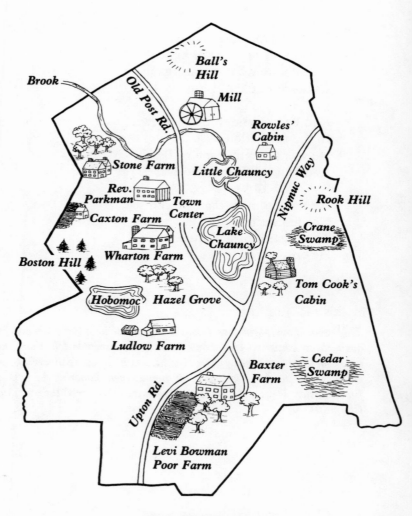

WESTBOROUGH
· 1779 ·

I . The Devil's Pact

TOM COOK SAT contentedly on a tree stump in front of the dilapidated trapper's cabin he now called home. He had simply moved in to the abandoned shack, knowing that it was of no concern to anyone. Tom's legs were spread apart comfortably, and he whittled slowly and carefully at a long, thin willow branch. The chips rose lazily in the air and settled softly on the ground between his bare feet. As he worked, the faint sound of crackling leaves reached his alert ears.

'Tis the sound of footsteps, he decided. Now, who could be this far out of town?

The sound became closer, but Tom did not move from his seat or look up from his whittling. The September sun had warmed his slight body from head to toe, and he felt as sluggish as a garden snake basking on a rock. If there's trouble ahead, it will find me no matter what I do, he thought, so there's no point in dashing about. From the corner of his eye, Tom saw a shadowy figure moving between the trees.

"You needn't spy on me," he said out loud. "I've nothing to hide."

A young boy emerged from the shade of the forest and stepped into the clearing near the shores of Lake Chauncy. He looked warily at Tom.

"You must be Jed Baxter's boy," Tom said with sudden recognition. The Baxters had bought a small farm to the south of the village and had spent the summer coaxing a late crop of corn from the stubborn soil. They were newcomers to Westborough, and Tom had observed them carefully to determine their needs for surviving the coming winter.

There were three more children in the family younger than the lad who stood before Tom, and he knew there was nothing to spare in their cabin.

"What's your name?" Tom asked. His soft blue eyes sized up the boy quickly, and then returned to look at the willow branch in his hand.

"Jesse," the boy answered simply. His voice was clear and strong. "I guess I must have gotten lost."

"Even newcomers don't get lost too easily around here," Tom countered evenly, a touch of annoyance in his voice. " 'Tis my guess your schoolmates have sent you here on a dare. Well, now that you've proven how brave you are, you'd better head for home straightaway. There's folks in this town who won't take kindly to you if they think you've taken up with the likes of me."

"I wanted to come," the boy said earnestly. "I'm not afraid of you."

Tom ignored the comment, although he knew well enough that it was fear that kept nearly everyone in the small Massachusetts town away from his door. "Get along, Jesse. I'm sure you've plenty of chores waiting to be done."

But Jesse stepped closer and looked with curiosity at Tom's whittling. "Pa's let me off chores a bit now that I'm going to school. He says getting some learning is the finest gift he's ever given me. I've already learned to write my name and tell the date. Look here."

Tom could not help taking an interest as Jesse settled himself at Tom's feet and scratched with a stone into the earth: "Jesse Baxter, September 12, 1779."

"You've a fine, neat hand," Tom praised him. As he watched Jesse's face from the closer vantage point, it did not seem timid, as he had first thought, but confident in a quiet way.

"School will fit you up to read the Bible," Tom offered,

"but I'd wager it won't teach you to whittle a flute as fine as this." He held out the willow branch for Jesse to see. The bark had been slid down from around the yellow wood, and small, even notches were carved along its length. Tom moved the bark back easily and placed the mouthpiece between his lips. A low and mellow tune floated through the trees and across the pond as he tested the instrument.

" 'Tis pretty enough to make the devil weep," Tom said.

At the mention of the devil, Jesse was visibly startled. He glanced about and shifted his legs nervously.

Tom observed the boy's every movement, judging his resolve, and ready to test him further. "Aye, the devil," he repeated with emphasis, leaning toward Jesse's face. Jesse did not flinch but met his steady gaze.

"I don't believe what people say about you," the youngster said quickly. Too quickly, to Tom's mind, as if he were trying to convince himself.

"And what do they say?" Tom baited him.

Jesse seemed to gather reassurance as he looked into Tom's smooth, unlined face and his deep blue eyes. He answered firmly, "They say you are in league with the devil."

Tom's face seemed to pale, if only for a moment. "Who's told you the tale? Is it the boys from school?"

"I know the bigger boys are just trying to scare me," Jesse said. "I don't believe none of it. And little Bess Ludlow told me about you being the Leveller. She says one day after haying, her family came back to their cabin and found a whole churn full of cream, just waiting to be turned into butter. She says her pa's told them stories about how you borrow the extra food from farmers that have more than they can use and secretly leave it in the homes of families that don't have enough. She says you try to level things off that way, but no one will tell if it's really you, or the sheriff will put you back in jail."

Jesse paused and looked at Tom, waiting for his reaction. But Tom did not say a word, and Jesse spoke up again. "Then the bigger boys came over and started teasing Bess and calling her a baby. They said Tom Cook is the devil's henchman and is nothing but a thief!"

"I've been called thief often enough, but 'tis by the likes of those who hoard their bounty and can't bear to see it shared. 'Tis families like the Stones and the Whartons, who turned their backs on me when I needed help the most. And as for the devil, I turn my back on him and give away all that I come by. I keep nothing for myself."

"There was more," Jesse said cautiously. "They said your own mother sold your soul to Beelzebub, the devil." Then the boy blurted out the question that Tom concluded was the reason behind the boy's visit. "Be it true? 'Tis an awful tale! I pray you tell me 'tis a lie!"

Tom did not answer right away. He reached into his back pocket, easing the flute in as far as it would go and pulling out a small leather-bound Bible. Its edges were rubbed smooth, and the gold lettering on the cover had nearly worn off. Tom placed the Bible on the ground between him and his young listener, trying to decide whether he would answer the question. As he opened the book's pages to the sky, he made his choice.

" 'Tis true, lad, but don't you fear. Old Beelzebub is not so clever as wily Tom Cook. I've lived by my wits all my life, and I'll not stop long enough for the Wicked One to catch me."

Tom leaned back against the cabin wall and went on in a soft voice, " 'Twas none of my mother's fault, you must understand. Why, my mother was a member of the great Forbush family and had never known the feeling of an empty larder. She brought as dowry the house Doc Horton lives in now, and my father brought to the marriage his trade as a blacksmith. There came ten children into the family as time went on, but Pa met troubles at every turn, and soon his living wasn't enough with so many mouths to feed. He took to brooding and leaving my mother for days at a time."

Tom continued. "My mother says I was but a tyke of three when the fever took me. She recollected my body was as hot as a red ember, and a worse case the doc had never seen. I could not swallow a morsel of food nor a drop of water, and my eyes were clouded so I did not seem to know her face."

Tom stopped for a moment, and the leaves in the clearing rustled in a sudden gust of wind, rose up in the air, and then fell whispering down upon the forest floor. Tom saw a shadow of fear cross Jesse's face.

"Pity my mother," he said. "Pa was off ramblin' again, and she had all the burden to bear. Not a soul came to her side except Reverend Parkman with his futile prayers and his solemn judgment that my illness showed God's wrath for Pa's shiftless ways. When the doc said he could do no more, Ma said she could not bear it."

Tom knew the tale was more than the boy had ever dreamed, but he did not stop. He felt a knot loosening in his chest as he shared his secret for the first time.

"Late one night," he went on, "in that blackness that seems to forbid the dawn to ever come, my mother says I took a turn for the worse. The end was at hand and could not be denied. All alone she sat, in a house empty of all except the sound of quiet breathing, without a word of comfort from another living soul. In fear and weakness she rose and cursed the Lord who made her sorry life. She swore she would give her soul if only she could save her boy."

Tom could see that Jesse was drawn into his tale, and the

boy edged closer to the open Bible on the ground, his eyes never leaving Tom's face.

"When a body swears like that, Beelzebub is never far. Just waiting for his beck and call, he comes to strike the deal. And so it was that awful night. A heavy knock shivered the door, and then old Beelzebub pulled the latchstring and entered where he had been called. My mother says he looked like a fancy gentleman going to a funeral, in a black velvet waistcoat and a black tricornered hat. The embers in the fire smoldered and then burst out in full flame as if a weathered log had been cast upon the grate. Then the Wicked One held out a gloved hand and spread upon the table a pact my mother must agree to, or lose her boy forever. Willing to endure the fires of hell for the sake of her son, my mother moved to sign her name in ink.

"But does the devil want that mother's soul? No!" Tom stamped his foot upon the earth with vengeance, and Jesse nearly fled. But Tom reached out a hand and touched the boy's shoulder gently.

" 'Tis fearsome worse than that. Old Beelzebub says he'll cure the boy, and protect him for all his life, but that he will claim his soul when it pleases him. My soul!" Tom shouted into the forest. "My own soul!"

Tom's shoulders slumped, and he paused and took a breath. "No mother could agree to such a pact. My mother took me in her arms to say the devil nay, but when she heard my low breathing and saw the limpness in my hand, she knew that she must give her son into the devil's care or lose him then and there. 'Spare his life!' she cried. 'Only spare his life, and I care not what he becomes!' She rose up from the bedside, took the pen in hand, and signed the devil's awful pact.

"The Wicked One vanished then, without a trace, and my mother wondered if it were a dream. But then she says I called her from my bed, and took a drink. By morning the fever was gone, and then she knew the deed that she had done.''

Tom rose from the stump and drew Jesse up to him. A sense of relief flooded him. '' 'Tis many years since that night, and the devil has come to me in many shapes to tempt me with food and riches. 'Tis said he can become a fox or squirrel, he can be youthful or knotted with old age, and I have heard his voice upon the wind. But I shall not be swayed by his temptations. 'Tis Beelzebub's bargain and none of my own.''

Tom slapped Jesse on the back, and he felt the boy relax. His face broke into a grin, and the spell of fear was broken. "I shall be the first man smart enough to outwit the devil himself, I promise you, lad. I've more than fish brains in this head of mine, and I'll not swallow any bait the devil dangles before me. A fish who can never be tempted can never be caught. You hear that, Beelzebub?''

Tom shook his fist in the air at the imaginary demon, and Jesse joined him in a good, long laugh. Tom looked closely at the boy once again. Perhaps he was just about the age Tom had been when he struck out on his own, and Tom noted that he seemed to have much of the same determination. He was certainly unlike the other boys in town, who would never venture near him.

"Come on, lad," Tom said. "I'll walk you up the road a ways. I've got work to do." With that, Tom pulled the willow flute from his pocket, slipped the Bible back in, and sauntered off from his cabin, never pausing to close the cabin door.

The pair soon parted ways, and Jesse set off down the Upton Road to his father's farm, while Tom headed up the Old Post Road piping a light tune through the kaleidoscope of colored leaves that overhung the path. He had some misgivings about having confided in the boy; yet he also felt strangely satisfied that Jesse had listened to his tale.

I've got to get my mind off that boy and think about making myself useful, he warned himself. He heard the honking of a flock of Canada geese overhead as they flew to their winter nesting grounds. Some might think that the warm September air meant the cold weather was still far ahead, but Tom knew better.

'Tis going to be an early winter, he decided. The animals always know. His bare feet slapped at the dust that covered the path leading toward the village mill. This section of Westborough was the site of the town's largest and most successful farms, and Tom felt that it would be fertile ground for collecting a few winter necessities.

The trees thinned out as Tom approached the homestead of Caleb and Hannah Stone. Tom never failed to be awed by the farm, no matter how many times he viewed it. The rough hills that dominated the Westborough landscape flattened out as they approached the Stones' rich meadows, as if to stretch themselves into submission for the benefit of the family's prosperity. Acres of apple orchards graced the gentle slopes that banked the meadows, and wild blackberry and blueberry bushes hugged the land.

Tom settled casually under one of the apple trees near the house and picked up a fallen apple that was only slightly bruised.

Horse fodder, he thought with annoyance as he bit into the sweet fruit. The fine lady Hannah Stone would never use a spotted apple for her pies, now would she? Oh, no! This is only fit for horse fodder!

Tom leaned back against the gnarled tree, letting the flies buzz around him and casting an eye to the homestead. A gigantic center chimney rose up through the roof and probably served an abundance of cozy fireplaces. Unlike most houses in town, which were unpainted, the Stones' house was stained red, as was a dainty picket fence set atop the stone wall that enclosed the herb garden in the front yard. That last detail of showiness always offended Tom the most.

As his eyes glanced over the red clapboards, they rested on a bright comforter draped over the window ledge, fat as a plump chicken flapping in the fresh air. *I can imagine the warmth that comforter could give a body on a cold night,* Tom thought with relish. *How many geese have given their warm down feathers to make it puff with pride?*

In a moment, Tom's quick wits had flashed out a plan. He tossed the apple core aside and sauntered up to the side of the house. With his head thrust back and his hands set jauntily on his hips, he looked up at the second-floor window and its beckoning prize. Then, with one hand on the trellis that clung to the side of the house, he scaled the wall as if he possessed cat claws instead of bare toes. Within a few inches of the window, he stretched out his arm and eased the comforter over the ledge. Its fullness swelled as he leaped silently down to the ground below.

Gathering the four corners into one hand, he slung the prize over his shoulder. Whistling merrily to himself, he marched back to the road, his feet slapping at the dust. Instead of making a quick escape, however, he turned in at the Stones' prim gravel path, stepped boldly to the heavy front door, and gave the brass knocker three sharp raps.

The door opened wide, and Tom saw Karen, the housekeeper, looking at him. Recognizing Tom, she quickly pushed the door closed until just a crack of sunlight lit her wide eyes.

"State your business, Tom," she demanded.

"Well, good day, missy," Tom began politely. "I'm just heading into town and find this here comforter a right heavy load. I'd be most grateful to you if you'd let me stash it here a mite till I can come back for it."

"Go your way, Tom. Lady Stone don't need to start no storage trade," was the abrupt answer.

It was just what Tom had expected. "I'll gladly give it to you, then, Karen. I can't tote it no more," he complained, and wiped his forehead with his sleeve. " 'Tis sure a fine piece for the coming cold nights. Even the geese have begun their flight from here. This will be an uncommon hard winter, for sure."

"Get on, I say," Karen retorted hotly. She peered at the comforter more closely through the crack in the door. "Do you know how many comforters, just like that one, are in this house? A body could smother on the coldest of nights. We don't need no comforters, and don't wish to set eyes on that one again!"

"Thank you, missy," said Tom, and he bowed ever so slightly. "I'll take the baggage and be off. You'll never be bothered with it again, I promise you."

"That's good news to me!" Karen shouted, and she slammed the door with a decisive *thud!*

Once again, Tom slung the comforter over his shoulder and headed back to the road, whistling his satisfaction into the sunny sky. He walked lightly with the bulky load, south toward the hills and Jed Baxter's rocky farm.

I've done nothing as yet for the Baxters, he thought, so perhaps I'll welcome them into the community with a comforter to protect the young ones from the winter drafts. He looked up toward the sun, sitting squarely overhead. It's just about noontime, I figure, and the Baxters almost always take a bit of bread and cider out in the fields when Jed is working. I can spread this piece on the bed and be gone before a soul knows anyone's been about.

As Tom walked down the path, the comforter seemed to

grow heavier and heavier until his strong back fairly bent with the weight. Soon it seemed an effort to whistle and walk at the same time.

As if on orders from an unseen commander, the wind began to rustle the trees, the sun clouded over, and the air grew damp and cold. We must be in for a storm, Tom thought. I'd best hurry on my way. Dark clouds rolled across the sky, and the distant rumble of thunder reached Tom's ears. He felt colder and colder, and his bare feet seemed to tread on frozen earth.

II · A Comforting Deed

WHAT A SUDDEN change in the fine weather, Tom mused. Shivers raced up his back and his teeth began to chatter. As Tom shuffled along the road, he thought again of the Canada geese hurrying to their nesting grounds, and he remembered that winter would soon be upon him.

Wouldn't this comforter be precious in my drafty cabin? His back began to warm where the blanket lay, and his mind imagined how cozy it would be to snuggle under its warmth on a snowy night. I've never had a piece like this in all my New England winters.

Slower and slower Tom walked, stronger and gustier blew the wind, and still the comforter weighed him down so that he seemed to move slower than maple sap on a January day. I must rest a moment, he decided, and he settled himself on a fallen log at the side of the road. How can this airy comforter sap my strength so? he wondered. It must be the force of the wind pushing against my stride. I shan't rest for long, though, for I must get to the Baxter's before the storm sends them all rushing back to the cabin.

Tom laid the bright comforter carefully on the ground beside him. As soon as he dropped it, the wind rose and blew coldly against his back. His hand hesitated in reaching for it again, as if an inner caution caused his indecision, but then he lifted the piece and draped it around his shoulders, covering his shivering back and his head as protection against the gusts of wind that blew at him mercilessly.

With the downy comforter pulled around him, Tom's body generated warmth, and he felt as if he had entered a warm cabin sheltered from the hostile elements. He forgot his intention to hurry to the Baxters' and nestled within his makeshift tent as if he would remain there forever.

Ah, such blessed warmth, he thought in ecstasy. I shall never get through the winter without this comforter.

The wind raged stronger about Tom's covered head, but he was lost in reverie until a dead tree limb snapped in the coming storm and crashed to the ground near his feet. Like a jackrabbit that suddenly smells a hungry fox, Tom leaped from his downy shelter, startled into awareness of what he was dreaming and the task before him.

What can I be thinking? he admonished himself. Why, I won't mind the cold. 'Tis the tykes who need to be tucked under this pile of goose feathers. Shame on me for my selfish thoughts!

Tom looked up at the threatening sky. This is too much even for New England's fickle weather. 'Tis a freak, it is, and I'd wager a king's ransom 'tis old Beelzebub tempting me again. "You'll not trap me for such a small price as this!" Tom shouted into the howling wind.

With determination, Tom shouldered the comforter once again and tried to hurry on his way. It now seemed less of a load, and his steps quickened. The wind began to settle, too, but the colorful maple trees along the path swayed and groaned.

As Tom turned in at the Baxters' stone wall, his resolution to give them the comforter was firm. The wind gave a lingering moan and died down. The clouds rolled back across the sky, and the sun shone forth.

The comforter had grown as light as it had felt when he began his journey, and in a moment, Tom was within sight of the Baxters' cabin. He slipped behind a stand of birch trees and tried to survey his chances for leaving the comforter on the children's bed without being noticed.

Jed Baxter was far behind the cabin, guiding his horse

and plow in straight furrows through the fields. Jesse trailed along behind, picking out the stones and casting them aside.

Outside the kitchen-room door, Baxter's wife rested a cake of brown soap on the edge of the wooden washtub and stood up, shaking out a last dripping shirt. How often Tom had seen his own mother bent over the same unending task. He could picture her still, and he realized how much he missed her.

Goody Baxter hung the shirt on a nearby rope that had been stretched between two sturdy trees. She called the younger children as she turned from the line, wiping her hands on a crisp white apron.

"Come, children," she called. "Your pa's waiting on his dinner! Samuel, fetch the dinner basket. Faith, you slice the bread I set on the board near the hearth. And Jonathan, you fetch a jug of cider from the cold cellar. Be quick now!" Her orders sent them scurrying to complete their tasks, and Tom knew that in a short time, the entire family would be out in the fields eating a light meal.

Such timing! he congratulated himself. Even though I tarried on the path, I've arrived just in time to have the whole cabin to myself. If there's one thing that is shared by all the farmers about, 'tis that they are so regular in their habits. That's one routine I'll never be trapped in! Folks can say many things about me, but never that I am predictable!

He smiled to himself and rubbed his hands together to shake the chill that had gripped them during the sudden wind. He settled down in the midst of the trees that hid him and watched until Goody Baxter and the children had trooped off to the fields with the basket of food, looking like a raggle-taggle parade.

With a chuckle of delight, Tom bounded out from his hiding place and dashed from one thick tree to another,

pausing at each one to listen for the sound of anyone approaching. But his caution was half-hearted, for he felt certain that the Baxters would not return to the cabin until after
their dinner had been eaten and the children had played in
the fresh furrows, searching for Indian spear points.

Although the cabin door was ajar, Tom headed for a side
window. After first peering in to be sure he was alone, he
tossed in the comforter, pulled himself to a sitting position
on the ledge, and then let his feet drop quietly onto the dirt
floor. He glanced around the cabin, noting the Baxters' bed
nestled in the corner. A trundle bed was slipped beneath it
and was pulled out at night for the younger children. Tom
glanced up and noticed that Jesse had been given a makeshift bed on the loft. It was open to the room below, but
Tom knew it was the coldest spot in the cabin. Perhaps, he
thought, Jesse can add the youngsters' old blanket on top of
his own, now that they will have the new one.

He stepped to the wooden bedstead and began pulling at
the trundle. A light patchwork coverlet was neatly tucked
over the muslin sheeting, and Tom could see that it con-
tained not an ounce of stuffing. He folded the coverlet
neatly and set it aside while he quickly worked to spread the
puffy comforter in its place. As soon as it was carefully
tucked in on each side, Tom stepped back to admire its
beauty. "Well, goodbye to this downy piece," he sighed,
"though I'm sure it finds a welcome home here."

Tom stooped to push the trundle bed back into its sheltered niche, but as he pushed, he found that the thickness of
the new comforter impeded its movement. He concentrated
on flattening it with one hand, while pushing his knee and
free hand at the trundle.

He was startled out of his concentration by a voice behind
him. "So, 'tis you!" Tom turned and saw Jesse standing in
the doorway, looking at him with a mixture of shock and ad-

miration. "I thought I saw someone slip in at the window. Don't worry, though. I didn't tell Ma."

"Jesse!" Tom blurted out. "What are you doing here? I just came to call and found no one at home."

"And so I suppose you decided to change the linens while you were here," Jesse laughed at him. "What have you got there, Tom?"

Tom knew he could think of a better excuse for his presence, but Jesse's eyes were so admiring, and his enjoyment at discovering the deed so evident, that Tom changed his mind.

"I'll be honest with you, Jess," he said. "I've brought a comforter for your brothers and sister. 'Tis all aired out and ready for the cold nights to come."

Jesse stepped over to the bed and fingered the plump comforter with its quilted ticking. " 'Tis as fine a piece as I've ever seen, Tom," he said. "Who can spare it?"

Tom's honesty flagged a bit at this direct question. If he told Jesse the comforter had come from the Stones', the boy could be made to tell his parents, or even the sheriff, how it had come to his cabin. They would both be safer if he did not know.

"I'll tell you this much," he said. "I'm told that where this comes from there are enough comforters to smother a body on the coldest of nights. The folks who had this piece don't wish to store it and say they don't wish to set eyes on it again." Once again Tom held the puffy comforter flat, and this time Jesse pushed the trundle back in place.

"Astonishin'!" Jesse exclaimed. "It would seem fitting that things be levelled off if they boast that many covers!"

Tom smiled at Jesse's choice of words. "My feelings exactly," he agreed. "And now, the Leveller must be off. I trust you not to tell a soul you saw me here." He gazed intently at Jesse, and saw his agreement as he nodded confidently.

"Wait!" the boy suddenly called as Tom turned to leave. "How about a cooling mug of cider before you go?"

"Cider?" Tom repeated in disbelief. "Why, I'm chilled to the bone from that wind. A bit of tea would be a blessing, though, if there's a pot boiling."

"Did you say wind?" Jesse asked. "Why, we've had nothing but bright sun and gentle breezes all the day." He turned to the fireplace. "Look, Ma's taken the kettle down on such a warm day. I can brew a pot in a twinkling."

"No, Jesse, I must get on before your whole family comes searching for you. No wind, you say?" he asked again. "That's odd. I sure hit a corker of a cold wind on my way here." He did not tell Jesse of his suspicions that the storm had been sent for his own personal torment, and the boy did not press him for an explanation. Tom thought there were some things best left unsaid.

"How can I thank you for the comforter, Tom?" Jesse asked.

"You can't thank me at all," Tom said lightly, tossing off the boy's gratitude like a coat that did not fit. " 'Tis not my bounty you share, and you've helped me hide the deed, to boot! But you can thank the rich families of this town when you say your prayers tonight. 'Tis lucky for the likes of us that there are some who have more than they can ever use."

With that, Tom slipped out the window, as if it were the most natural way to leave, and headed up the path. Slender white birch trees cast lengthening shadows across the road as he headed back toward the woods to check on a few newly laid traps and to see if the hazel nuts had begun to ripen. 'Tis time to set up a store of food for myself, he thought. He noted with satisfaction that his traps were well hidden and that there was some sign of activity around them. He would begin to check them each day.

As the afternoon drew to a close, he decided that on the morrow he would gather the hazel- and beechnuts that had begun to ripen, and perhaps lay in a supply of fallen apples from the Stones' expansive orchards. He headed for home wrapped in thoughts of meager days ahead, when the fruits of the land would not be there for the taking. He turned and cut through the back pastures of the James Wharton farm, looking for a shorter way home before darkness fell. This will lead me right to my door, and to a quicker supper, he reckoned. I'm near starved! Wharton may not like having Tom Cook in his pastures, but he surely can't condemn a man for merely passing through.

The cows in the pasture sent up a chorus of mooing as Tom approached their domain, but they did not pause in their chewing. James Wharton had enjoyed the good fortune of seeing his herd of prize Herefords multiply each year since he had first sailed from England with a few chosen cows and bulls, which had only narrowly survived the hazardous voyage across the ocean.

Tom's father had always marveled that the man had such foresight to know that with a built-in supply of meat, milk, butter, and cheese, he could take his time clearing the land and waiting for the crops to yield their first harvest. From the start, neighboring settlers filled the dairyman's coffers with goods and coin in return for his rich dairy products.

Now, Tom surveyed the success of Wharton's plans. Besides the livestock that grazed in the lush meadows, sheep dotted the grassy hillsides. Plump chickens and bright-plumed bantam roosters strutted cockily through the yard. Lazy brood sows wallowed in the still-warm mud, their squealing piglets snuggled beneath their ample bodies.

When you own a farm like this one, Tom reflected, you

needn't worry about winter meals. There is milk from the cows and ham from the hogs, and all the eggs and chickens you can eat. The homestead loomed ever larger before him, and soon Tom forgot his empty stomach and his desire to return home and found his feet turning toward the threshold.

III · In Pudding Time

DINNER WAS COOKING in the fireplace, and its fragrance tickled Tom's nose as well as his fancy. Silent as a cat on padded feet, he crept cautiously to the open window of the kitchen-room. A tremendous stone fireplace dominated one wall, and heavy iron pots hung from every hook. Bouquets of drying herbs hung by their stems across the brick wall, waiting to spice the stews and meats the gaping fireplace would cook.

Cynthia, the Whartons' long-time servant, was pouring boiling water into a pot hung over the fire. Steam engulfed the kettle until she set the lid on tightly once again.

Tom's eyes widened at the sight. Steamed pudding! He marveled at his sudden good fortune and chuckled silently to himself. Why, I have surely come in pudding time!

His roving eye took in the feast Cynthia was preparing, and he noticed her young daughter, Tessie, who cooed happily as she rolled a shiny horse chestnut across the floor. Cynthia had been taken in by the Whartons when she was ten years old as an indentured servant. She was to serve them as housemaid and receive food, clothing, and a warm room in return. She had since married one of Wharton's farm hands, but Wharton insisted that she continue in his service until the contracted age of eighteen.

A plump chicken roasted on a spit over the blazing fire, and its dripping juices set off a chorus of hisses from the flames below. Stuffed venison was taken from the beehive oven, and hot loaves of crusty bread were set alongside the succulent meat to await slicing by the master.

A smaller pot bubbled over the hearth fire, and when

Cynthia stirred its contents, Tom's eyes feasted on a mouth-watering blend of carrots, turnips, and potatoes glazed with honey.

All this, and a pudding, too! Tom thought in amazement. The Whartons must truly be gluttons to cook up such a meal. And they never see fit to give away so much as a drop of milk. Tom had never known Wharton to offer a helping hand to anyone without receiving something in return.

He thought of the Ludlows, who lived in a small cabin just south of the Wharton homestead. Noah Ludlow farmed his land as best he could, each year clearing more acreage, and he worked for Wharton to supplement his insufficient harvest. With eight young mouths to feed, the Ludlows never seemed to keep from the edge of hunger.

Yet Wharton never offered Noah a farthing more than the agreed-upon wage for a day's labor, and he never shared his own bounty, no matter how bad times were for his neighbor.

This year, Tom knew the Ludlows had started a small brood of setting hens, and he hoped that would be the beginning of a better fortune for them and provide independence from the likes of families like the Whartons.

Suddenly, Wharton pushed through the door into the kitchen-room, and Tom flattened himself against the side of the house.

"The reverend has arrived, Cynthia," he declared importantly, "and I must remind you that everything is to be served according to my instructions." Tom peered cautiously in at the window's edge, to see Wharton pulling his velvet vest down over his protruding belly and tugging at the ruffles at his cuffs so that they showed fully at his coat sleeves.

Wharton glared at Cynthia, who was busily stirring the

vegetables, until she turned and curtsied with a meek, "Yes, sir. Everything is just as you instructed, sir."

Wharton turned abruptly on his heel, satisfied with Cynthia's deference to his position, and began to stride out of the room, when his shoe landed squarely on Tessie's horse chestnut and his foot slid out from under him. His heavy body jerked gracelessly, his arms waving in the air, until he caught his balance by leaning against the hearth wall. His face reddened.

"See that you get this place tidied up immediately!" he bellowed. "You're a disgrace!"

"Yes, sir," said Cynthia, bowing her head low, but Tom observed the smile that stole across her face to see Wharton dance about so.

A puckish grin stole across Tom's face, as well. *Wharton insists that everyone live up to the expectations he has of them,* he thought. *Well, I shall be no exception, Master Wharton, for this wily leveller has hatched a plan that will not surprise you at all.*

A bell tinkled insistently in the depths of the household, and Cynthia began scurrying about the kitchen, setting food on platters and reaching into the cold cellar for a bottle of wine. She tidied her hair, smoothed down her starched apron, and primly carried the tray of steaming, golden-brown chicken into the dining hall.

Tessie watched her mother's retreating back and let out a wail, crawling unhappily toward the door. Tom knew he had but a moment to act. Pulling himself in through the open window, he landed softly on the polished floor. In two quick steps, he was at the hearth. The sound of Wharton's gravelly voice pierced his ears as the gentleman chided his servant.

"Can't you keep that wailing child still?" he demanded. "I agreed to let you marry, Cynthia, and granted you leave to keep the child with you at your chores, but I won't put up with that crying and wailing!''

"I'm sorry, sir,'' came Cynthia's soft voice. "She gets frightened when I leave her. She don't know it's just for a moment.''

Lifting the cover from the pudding pot, Tom thrust his hand toward the steaming kettle and drew the pudding bag out by its knotted end. Without a sound, he deftly set the heavy lid back in place.

Reverend Parkman's voice now reached Tom's ears. "The sound of God's children is never unpleasant,'' the clergyman declared.

With sixteen children of his own, Tom thought, he should know. Yet he is dining here, and they are all at home.

"She's just a baby, James,'' soothed Priscilla Wharton. "She'll grow out of it.''

"Grow out of it?'' bellowed Wharton. "Before you know it, the tyke will be walking in with Cynthia, clinging to her legs and spilling the soup!''

So that's the master's view, Tom reflected. 'Tis my guess that by the time little Tess is walking about, Cynthia will be eighteen and Wharton will neither see nor hear either of them about the place. With the scalding bag held safely at arm's length, Tom handed something to the crying Tessie and let himself back out through the window into the darkening evening.

He crept silently along the back of the house toward the barns, and held his breath as two idle farmhands passed not far from him into the horse stalls. "I smell a puddin'!'' one of the men declared with relish, sniffing at the air. Tom realized that the strong aroma of steamed beef mixed with sweet molasses and cider had filtered through the cloth bag into the air. He could smell rare spices of cinnamon and nutmeg

as if the pudding were set on a plate before him. He lowered
the bag toward the ground, hoping the men would not follow the scent.

"Do you think Cynthia will slip us a bit of the leftovers?"
the second man wondered aloud.

"Not a chance," replied the first man with disappointment as the pair disappeared into the barn. "I'd wager that
Wharton even counts the bread crusts before he parcels
them out to his hounds."

Tom moved quickly past the barn door, and as he safely
reached the far side of the house, he heard Wharton's voice
reverberating through the air from the dining-hall window.
Cynthia must have just reported that the pudding pot is
empty, Tom thought gleefully. I wonder if she also men-
tioned that Tessie is sucking on a peppermint stick? Wharton was standing at the table gesturing with rage, and his
wife and the reverend were trying to settle him down.

"I don't know what could have happened to it," Priscilla
Wharton said, "but bless the Lord that we've more than
enough for dinner without the pudding. I don't think we'll
ever find out what happened to it, so don't trouble yourself,
James, dear."

"Trouble myself!" he stormed. "I'd swear the cowardly
deed can be laid at Tom Cook's door. I would spare no trouble if only I could rid myself of that plague of a thief!"

"Let us pray for his soul and give thanks for our bounty," offered Reverend Parkman solemnly.

Tom did not wait for their blessing but ran swiftly across
the fields, laughing like a demon and heading straight for
the Ludlows' cabin. Tom ran as fast as his legs would carry
him, anticipating the delight with which Noah's family
would greet the rich pudding.

From behind him, Tom heard the sound of barking dogs
giving him chase. 'Tis Wharton's hounds, he thought with

dismay. He turned his head to judge the distance of the approaching dogs, and as he did so, his foot caught on a thick tussock of grass, and Tom went sprawling down upon the ground, his head hitting the hard earth.

For several minutes, Tom could not open his eyes; he lay back, dizzy and panting. The hounds had stopped their barking and were licking playfully at Tom's face. Tom realized that he still held the pudding bag in his hand, and he thought that perhaps the dogs were begging for a taste of the mincemeat. But the dogs had picked up a more challenging scent, and as Tom struggled to sit up and clear his head, a covey of partridges rose flapping from the grass as the dogs flushed them out.

Peeping shrilly in alarm, the partridges flew past Tom in panic, with the hounds in swift pursuit. The sun had dropped behind the surrounding hills, and the darkness grew heavier, but Tom could not yet move on. His head ached and swam dizzily. The aroma of the spicy pudding grew stronger as Tom pulled it protectively closer. Just one slice of this mincemeat would be a feast fit for kings and princes. He shook his head to dispel his dizziness, but his mind seemed to grow foggier as the pudding steamed from the bag before him.

"Peep-it! Peep-it!" squawked the patridges as they tried to find a hiding place in the tall grasses, and to Tom's confused mind, they seemed to say, "Eat-it! Eat-it!"

Perhaps I might just have a taste, Tom thought to himself. What harm would it do? I have gone to a terrible lot of trouble to capture this feast for the Ludlows, but I could surely reward myself with just a morsel and still have more than enough left for all of them. Tom set the bag down carefully on the grass.

"Eat-it! Eat-it!" chirped the partridges, and the wind picked up the command and whispered it loudly through the evening air. Tom's stomach rumbled in its emptiness and seemed to be growling its agreement to the plan.

Without a thought or care, Tom found himself struggling to loosen the pudding bag knot. He felt he must taste it or he would perish of hunger and longing. As his fingers struggled with the tight cotton, the hounds, tired of their game with the partridges, came bounding back, whining and yowling at the pungent smell of beef dripping with juices.

"Be off!" Tom scolded the animals, but they began to bark more loudly than ever at Tom's denial of the feast, and Tom saw lantern lights in the distance. A plague on the beasts, Tom thought. They've roused Wharton's farmhands to see what all the yapping is about. Upon my soul, I must be gone!

Suddenly, Tom's head was as clear as the violet night. My soul! he chided himself. What kind of pudding head am I that I can forget my soul for a morsel of meat?

Tom glared at the pudding bag and cursed his own weakness. 'Tis the devil trying to trap me again. "Will you never leave me in peace, Beelzebub?" Holding the bag firmly in front of him, he marched forward without hesitation, leaving the partridges, the dogs, and his temptations behind.

At the Ludlows' cabin, Tom peeked in through the doorway, which stood slightly ajar to clear the air in the small dirt-floored room. Two candles glowed on the long oak trestle table as Kate Ludlow spooned a thick soup into the wooden bowls set before each of the children. Noah had before him a loaf of hot bread, and he carved it into thin slices.

'Tis a poor meal for those who work so hard, Tom thought. He tried to decide the best way to give the pudding to the family without making it seem like charity. He had already been caught once today and did not want to repeat the misfortune.

He set the pudding bag down behind the cabin door and

ran around to the back of the house, near the low chicken coop. Cupping his hands to his mouth, he let out a high-pitched yowl and several low yips. He repeated the trick once more and then hid behind a tree.

"Foxes!" he heard Noah announce to the family in a stern voice. "Better see to the chickens!"

The entire family rose immediately from the benches and headed to the chicken coops. As Goody Ludlow followed her brood outside the house, Tom scooped up the pudding bag and slipped into the cabin. Quickly, he set a large pot on a hook over the dying fire. He stirred up the embers with a poker until they glowed and flamed. Then he set the pudding bag into the pot and poured the tea kettle full of boiling water over it.

In the wink of an eye, he was out the door again, disappearing into the shadow of a nearby boulder. Blessings to God that I go home to a bit of tea and bread, he reflected. It may not be mincemeat, but 'tis honest fare, nourishing to the body and better by far for the soul.

Tom did not move a muscle as he watched the Ludlows troop back into the kitchen-room, relieved to find that their stock was safe. He smiled contentedly as he saw their excitement when the steaming bag of pudding was discovered bubbling in the pot.

"Bless God," he heard Goody Ludlow murmur in astonishment. "Where in heaven did this bounty fall from? Even the bag is made of fine cotton ticking and not our rough muslin."

"I don't know," Noah said slowly, stroking his beard, "but I'd wager the whole bag that it has little to do with heaven and quite a lot to do with the Leveller."

"The Leveller! The Leveller!" chorused the children, hugging each other and jumping up and down at the prospect of a whole pudding for dinner.

Bess caught hold of her sisters' hands and danced around the room, singing, "Little Tommy Tucker must sing for his supper, but our Tommy Cook just takes it off the hook!"

Tom wished he could join in their dance, but he was satisfied to feel part of their happiness as he watched from his hiding place. The children's laughter echoed in his ears as he crept back toward the road, as did their chorused prayer as they gave thanks to the Lord for their good fortune and their good friend.

IV · Morning Light

TOM WAS AWAKE before the sun's warming rays filtered through the chinks in the cabin walls. He padded across the cold earth floor to stir up the fire and threw a heavy maple log across the embers to warm the drafty room. Still, he could not complain about the drafts, for the cabin was surely the most comfortable one he had found in his many moves around the village.

The trapper who owned it arrived with the first thaw in spring and left at the end of each summer, heading north to Canada for the colder months. This was the third year Tom had settled into the cabin as soon as its owner moved on. It was furnished with a low wooden bed, a washbasin and stand, a table and chair, and a few pots and utensils. Tom was always careful to leave the cabin in good order when spring arrived, and he frequently left behind a stack of firewood to show his thanks for use of the shelter. The trapper did not know who occupied his cabin in his absence, but when he left, the door was always unlocked.

Tom unrolled an extra blanket he had stored under the bed and removed the blue wool stockings and homespun brown vest that he had wrapped in it. 'Tis stocking weather, he thought as he perched on a low stool by the fire. He pulled the stockings on slowly, savoring their warmth and not minding their itching a bit. He looked at them with satisfaction. These may not be fine white silk like Reverend Parkman's, but they surely do know how to be a comfort to Tom Cook's cold feet!

He reached across the hearth for his boots. Their worn black leather was polished with care, and they slipped easily over Tom's stockings as if they remembered the terrain. Tom rose from the stool and took his muslin shirt from a peg near the fireplace. The heat from the burning log had curled into the coarse fibers, and warmth enveloped him as he drew it on. He smoothed the loose-fitting shirt into his trousers and then lifted his suspenders from an adjacent peg.

Leather straps looped through the well-worn suspender holes in Tom's pants, and he shrugged them up over his shoulders. Finally, he slipped into his long vest, and his outfit was complete.

From an oak barrel just outside the cabin door, he ladled a small amount of water into a black iron kettle and set it to boil over the fire. He poured a second ladleful into the blue washbasin. Cupping his hands, he plunged them down into the cold water, splashed his face quickly, and then groped around for a cloth to wipe the coldness from his face.

That will wake a body up, he chuckled to himself. It won't be many weeks before I'll have to break a layer of ice from the water barrel to wash my face.

The water in the kettle spewed steam, and Tom set out a tin mug and a brown teapot on the small table nestled against the wall. Holding the kettle with his face cloth, he gingerly poured most of the water into the teapot and then added the last few drops to the icy water in the washbasin.

Tom set to shaving the stubble from his face while the tea steeped. He took great pleasure in shaving each day, simply because no one had ever shown him how. Pa had moved long before a hair ever met my chin, he thought, but I've always been a good teacher to myself.

He recalled clearly the day his family had moved from Westborough. The fear of many townspeople that Tom was in league with the devil had grown stronger over the years. Any bit of success I ever had was seen as the devil's hand,

Tom thought bitterly. Ma had to teach me to read and write at home, for they wouldn't let me go to the schoolhouse with the other children.

"Tom Cook's the devil's son," they chanted at me. How could Pa make a living when few of the farmers dared enter his blacksmith shop? The family had to move to get a fresh start, Tom reassured himself. If I had gone with them, the tale would have followed us all. This was a debate he had held with himself frequently over the years, and he had rehearsed well all the reasons why he might have gone with them but had decided instead to remain behind.

Tom's image looked back at him seriously from the strip of tin that hung on the wall and served as a mirror. He forced an impish grin as he tied his long brown hair behind in a club-tail. A slim bit of leather served as a fastener, for Tom disdained the fashionable satin ribbons that adorned the white wigs of many of the town's gentlemen.

With a kick at the door latch and a strong arm, Tom heaved the shaving water out of the cabin door and at last sat down to his morning tea. As he dipped a leftover slice of dry bread in the steaming brew, a soft knock sounded at the door.

"Ho, Tom," called a low voice. " 'Tis me, Jesse. Are you awake?"

Tom opened the door with surprise and greeted his new friend. The boy was dressed in a starched white shirt and a broad-brimmed hat, and his face was shiny clean. "Awake?" he laughed. "I'll have you know I've beat that lazy sun by an hour! What are you doing here so early, and dressed like a fine gentleman, too?"

"I'm heading to Meeting," Jesse said proudly. Tom had not kept track of the days for a long time but realized it was Sunday. "I stopped in to bring you a few apples. We've such a bountiful crop, Pa says 'tis a good sign that the farm will prosper for us."

Tom laid the apples out on the table and smiled as the first beams of sunlight played across their red roundness. "I almost had a thought to cut them up and dry them in the sun, but they're just too pretty. I'd wager you've shined up every one of them," Tom teased, and Jesse's sheepish look confirmed his guess. "Set yourself down and have some tea."

Jesse pulled over the stool from the fireplace but declined to take the tea. "I can only stay a mite," he said. "You should have seen Ma last night when she pulled out the trundle and spied that comforter. She was truly dazzled, and I acted just as surprised as anyone. The children babbled about it all the morning. 'Tis a prize comforter, without a doubt."

There was silence then, as Tom sipped his tea in embarrassment. The farmers were reluctant to acknowledge the booty Tom distributed, for fear of being reprimanded at Meeting for encouraging his deeds and sharing in his "thievery." Yet Tom knew their gratitude by their silence, and he never expected thanks.

Jesse looked at Tom with hesitation, then spoke. "Don't you get lonely, living all by yourself? Where's your family?"

Tom had never discussed his family with anyone, but he felt he wanted Jesse to know what had happened. "I've told you how most folks believed I was bewitched," he began. "Somehow, the tale frightened people more as I got older. Soon people were afraid to come near any of the family, and Pa could not make a living. When I was about your age, they decided they had to have a fresh start, and planned to move up to Douglass. I couldn't bear to be a burden on them any longer, and determined it was time to strike out on my own.

Perhaps 'tis the devil's hold that makes me stay, but I choose to think it was my decision to stay in this town and prove I live by the Bible. It's given purpose to my life, and I like to think I help many folks in this town."

Tom reflected a moment. "I've learned to live by my wits, and I've learned that it was always the rich folks, who made such a show of going to Meeting, who treated me the worst. They never lent an understanding ear or a word of forgiveness to my mother and never lent a helping hand when I needed their charity the most."

"You don't have to be so alone," Jesse offered. "You could make friends with the farmers you've helped. They'd trust you."

"No, Jess. I won't be accepted in this town unless I stand before the Meeting and confess that the devil's led me to steal and ask the forgiveness of the Meeting. I'll never do it. I'm serving God in my own way and don't need anyone's blessing."

Tom stared down at his mug of tea. "I don't give myself time to be lonely. I'm busy trying to ease the life of those who have it hard and keep their empty larders from bringing the devil to their door too. 'Tis enough to occupy a lifetime, don't you think?" Tom looked up and smiled, but he sensed that he did not hide his feelings very well. The boy seemed to look deep within him, to hidden places where his feelings had long been stored and left undisturbed.

"Well, I'd like to be your friend," Jesse offered, "and I'm going to help you get by. I'm going to come by every morning and help you prepare for winter. I'm powerful at chopping wood. Please let me, Tom."

Tom stared at the boy's eager face. No one had ever made such a proposal to him before. He shook his head in disbelief. "You come to help me! Now, ain't that a warm way to start a cold morning!"

"You're always doing for others," Jesse said. "You've got to have a store of your own before winter."

"Well, Jesse, I've had the very same thought," Tom answered. "This morning, while you're listening to Reverend Parkman's golden words, I'll be out in the woods filling up a bag of hazelnuts." Tom drained off the last draught of tea. "I've got to get an early start to beat the squirrels and chipmunks, or there'll be nary a nut left for me."

Tom felt uncomfortable with the boy's offer and tried to dismiss it. "You're a fine lad for your thoughts, but you'd better be off to Meetin' before you're late and they throw you in the stocks." He opened the door, and Jesse followed him across the threshold. Instead of the morning silence outside the cabin, Tom looked up the path toward the sound of hoofbeats echoing through the woods. With frosty breath forming vapor in the cool air, two horses and two riders pulled up their reins at Tom's cabin.

"Ho, Sheriff!" Tom called, as the town's constable and his deputy dismounted. "What brings you out this way?"

The sheriff spoke haltingly, trying to regain his breath from the ride and trying to hide his nervousness at confronting the wily Tom.

" 'Tis a sad duty that I have, Thomas Cook, to arrest you for thieving victuals from the home of James Wharton. He does accuse you, and I must hold you in the jail till the quarrel be resolved."

"Thieving?" Tom said mockingly, looking up at the husky constable. "I've never stole so much as a button! 'Tis Wharton, with his overabundance, who steals from the poor their chances to get ahead in this world."

"I won't argue with you," the sheriff said, looking about him somewhat nervously. He spied Jesse standing near the cabin door and lowered his eyebrows disapprovingly. "You must come with me and settle this dispute before the Justice of the Peace. Doc Horton is Justice now, and he always deals with fairness.''

Fairness? Tom thought bitterly. It was Doc Horton who had bought his family's home for a pittance when they were forced to leave town. Tom would never forgive him for taking advantage of his parents' plight. Every time he passed the fine plaster house where he had been born and thought of someone else living there, he felt a surge of anger and misery. He would never let Doc Horton sit in judgment of him!

"Tom!" cried Jesse in alarm, breaking into Tom's thoughts. "You can't go to jail!"

Tom's smile never faded. "Don't worry your head, Jesse, lad. The jail has never been built that can hold Tom Cook."

Then Tom turned and eyed the heavyset sheriff. "Do I walk or ride this fine morning? I can surely keep pace with these old nags, and I don't want to overload your mount."

"These mares are as strong and fit as any in this fledgling country," countered the sheriff with indignation. "My horse can carry both of us, and you'll ride behind me. I know your wily ways, Tom Cook," he added, "and I'll bind your hands before we go."

"Behold the thieving criminal," Tom laughed, and held his hands dutifully in front of him while the sheriff bound them with a length of rope.

"Do you fear me that much?" Tom asked quietly, but the sheriff did not meet his eyes or offer him an answer.

The two lawmen mounted their horses, and Tom jumped up behind the sheriff, his hands bound together, his lithe body balancing with the horse's gait. As the men turned to head up the path, Tom gave a wink to his startled young friend, who seemed too astonished to move.

V · Sleight of Hand

THE HORSES LOPED stiffly up Old Post Road, their heads bobbing in rhythm with the tapping of their hooves against the rough road. The constable and his deputy rode silently, their faces stern, but Tom whistled gaily into the dappled sunshine, and the many-colored leaves overhead seemed to dance to his tune.

All the while Tom whistled, his mind was busy hatching a plan to save himself from jail. It wasn't the first time one of the town's prominent citizens had had Tom thrown in jail for stealing. I've know the inside of this jail before, he thought, and I'll not be placed there again.

In order to escape from the sheriff, Tom knew, he would first have to win his confidence, or at least force him to let down his guard. The sheriff was a large, ungainly man, and his wits were fit for little besides watching over defenseless drunkards, but Tom knew he took his position seriously, and Tom would have to act with caution.

"Sure is a mighty fine morning," Tom said innocently. "The sun is taking the chill off the air already."

"Yep," was the sheriff's terse reply.

"A body would think that winter would never come, but I've seen signs to the contrary."

"Signs?" asked the sheriff. Tom sensed that he had gotten his captor's attention.

"Sure signs. Just yesterday, 'twas, I saw the squirrels packing acorns into their cheeks with frantic energy. Up and down the trees they ran, never stopping for a moment. The geese have already begun their journey to winter nesting grounds, much earlier than usual. 'Tis going to be an uncommon hard winter ahead.''

"You think so?'' queried the sheriff with interest.

"No question about it. I predict that this winter is going to be long and fearsome. We'll not get about without sleds and rackets to help us. Have you begun to lay in a store of vittles for yourself and your family, Sheriff?''

Tom's coaxing warmed the sheriff's tongue, and soon he began relating his plans for the winter and telling how his wife and daughters had been working to preserve vegetables and stock up the cold cellar in anticipation of the short food supply ahead.

All the while the sheriff talked, Tom kept up an interested chorus of "Ayuh," and "Sure enough," and all the while the sheriff talked, Tom thought of how he would escape. The deputy rode just ahead of the sheriff's horse and never glanced back. Tom concluded that the animated conversation he heard convinced the deputy that everything was going smoothly.

Tom tested the rope on his wrists. It was loose enough so that he could move his fingers freely, and even move his hands a bit. He glanced down and noticed that a second rope was tied securely to the saddlebags. One end dangled loosely, while the rest of its coiled length was strapped in tightly.

"With my sons growing so fine, there's few chores I have to take to myself,'' the sheriff was saying.

"Ayuh, fine boys they are," lied Tom. Everyone knew the sheriff's sons were the biggest bullies in the town. "Fine young men.''

"A great comfort and help to their mother, too. Why, my Jonah can chop and stack a cord of wood in half a day.''

"Don't say?'' marveled Tom. "Now how old be your Jonah?''

The sheriff rattled on now, barely pausing long enough to hear Tom's few words of encouragement. He was lost in the sound of his own voice and in bragging about his family, and Tom felt pleased that the sheriff's misplaced pride would be punished with the loss of his prisoner. Still, it would take some time, and he had to be patient.

Pretending to be fascinated with the sheriff's description of his wife's cooking, Tom picked up the free end of the extra rope and gently threaded it through the sheriff's belt. He tied the rope securely in a tight knot, all the while encouraging the lawman's boasting with an occasional "My, my" and several "Mm-hmms."

When the knot was secure and the sheriff safely bound to his saddle, Tom spoke up. "No offense to your horse, Sheriff, but her gait's a mite rough, and I am being bounced to oblivion! I can barely keep my seat. Would it be a bother to you if I rode behind the deputy the rest of the way?"

"If it please you," agreed the sheriff cordially, warming up to Tom for all his agreeable listening. He pulled his horse to a stop and called to the deputy to do the same. "Here, Tom, let me help you down."

"No help required by a wiry man such as myself, Sheriff," Tom put in quickly. He slipped easily from his perch and approached the deputy's horse. The constable kept an eye on his prisoner as he pulled himself up.

"I almost thought you called yourself a 'wily' man," the sheriff confided to Tom with a guffaw. "You certainly are wiry, though. How many men could mount a horse with their hands tied together?"

Tom sensed that his attention and interest in the sheriff's family and well-being had totally taken down the lawman's apprehensions. He now displayed a new trust in his prisoner, just as Tom had hoped.

Once Tom was seated, he gave a nod to the pompous

sheriff. "I'll give my horse her rein," the sheriff called to the deputy. "Just let yours ride easy with the double load."

The constable's mare took the lead, and without a bit of coaxing the lanky deputy started talking Tom's ear off about his career as a lawman and how he would be sheriff himself one of these days.

Tom observed the deputy closely. He had always thought of himself as thin and would make jokes to himself about his pants falling down without the help of his suspenders, but sitting behind the deputy, he realized how skinny a man could be. He looks as though he's wearing a barrel held up by two ropes, Tom laughed to himself. The joke led Tom to a more serious thought. He surely wouldn't get far without those suspenders of his, now would he? But the deputy continued to chatter and his voice brought Tom back to the business at hand.

Tom guessed the deputy had been jealous of the lively conversation that had been going on behind him. Now that the prisoner was in his charge, he seemed to feel it was his turn to be heard. Tom was careful to be respectful so the deputy would not be influenced by stories he might have heard about Tom's evil ways.

Nimbly and stealthily, Tom turned his attention to the rope that tied his hands. With his free fingers, he began to pick at the weak knot patiently and with determination.

On and on chattered the deputy, as shrill as a bluejay, telling Tom his life story. He related how he had come to settle in Westborough and expressed his plans for a successful future—a future that did not in any way include the present sheriff.

" 'Tis a smart man that you are, Deputy," Tom encouraged the pock-faced young man. "I'd bet you're quite the ladies' man, as well. I'd wager there's not a maid about who wouldn't wish to be part of that promising future."

That was all the deputy needed to hear, and he was instantly launched on a discussion of all the young ladies of the town, which ones favored him the most, and the difficulty he was having in deciding which one to take for a wife.

Through all the boasting, Tom continued to work at the rope, and with several more cautious picks and one last gentle pull, his hands were free, and the rope that bound him was now in his hands and not around them. Tom let the rope slip down to the path, where it blended into the fallen leaves as perfectly as a snake. Tom never paused in his professed admiration of the deputy until he had lightly unbuttoned the two loops at the back of the suspenders that held up the young braggart's britches.

Briefly, the trio rode on, while Tom savored the moment to come. He took pride in the fact that his touch had been so light that neither the sheriff nor the deputy had noticed his movements any more than they might have felt the landing of a mosquito on their arm. As they approached a long hedge of wild roses, Tom pictured the mosquito in his mind's eye and laughed out loud when he thought of the sudden sting and the lasting itch that remains long after the insect has flown away.

The sheriff turned and slowed his horse at the sound of Tom's long laugh. "Well, gentlemen," the prisoner announced, "it has been a lovely morning's ride, and the conversation has been most memorable, but I have work to be done, and I'm afraid I can waste no more time with you." Tom slid quickly off the deputy's horse, waved good day to the startled lawmen, and slipped through a barely noticeable opening in the thorny bushes into the forest.

"After him!" yelled the sheriff, and he turned his horse and urged her forward. Tom glanced behind him as he walked and saw the sheriff's horse balk and then rear up at the thorny barrier. Instead of pursuing his prisoner, the sheriff suddenly found himself tossed from his seat and hanging from his saddle in midair. He looks like a ham hanging from the rafters of a smokehouse, Tom thought with amusement.

The sheriff's arms waved frantically in the air, unable to reach back to the saddle horn to steady himself. His legs kicked above him, trying to find solid ground. His surprised horse, uncertain what was expected of her, tossed her head with a whinny and backed away from the thorny underbrush into the path, trying to shake off the heavy load.

"Help!" yelled the sheriff, his face turning red, either from shame or from hanging upside-down.

Tom was now observing the comical confusion from a limb high up in a nearby maple tree. 'Tis a regular Punch and Judy show, he thought with delight. Hidden from view by the mottled green, orange, and yellow leaves, Tom imagined that the colorful foliage was a calico curtain framing the stage below and that the show was sent for his own personal entertainment.

The deputy was confused by the demands of the moment. He looked from the woods to the dangling sheriff and back again. He jumped down from his horse and began to race toward the woods, when he suddenly felt his pants dangling dangerously low. The deputy paused, yanking at his runaway britches and groping behind him for his flapping suspenders.

"Curse the blasted little devil!" shouted the sheriff. The deputy must wonder whether his boss is referring to himself or to me, Tom thought. He watched as the deputy pulled up his pants with one hand and attempted to assist the red-faced constable with the other.

"He's long gone by now, I fear, sir," offered the deputy disconsolately.

"And let him be!" shouted the sheriff in a rage. "The

man is protected by the devil, and I can't be expected to hold a man such as that. He's bewitched, he is!''

From his private box seat, Tom held his sides trying to remain silent, but it was one feat he could not accomplish. He burst into a fit of uncontrollable laugher, nearly tumbling from his lofty perch.

To the sheriff and the deputy, now standing in confusion in the middle of the road, the sound of laughter filtering through the air overhead must have seemed an eerie omen. They mounted their horses with dispatch and headed toward town.

What will they ever tell Wharton now? Tom wondered. Perhaps they will say that the devil lifted me right through the air, while they were stuck fast to their saddles. 'Tis another good story that will save them from admitting their foolishness and will excite all the wagging tongues that carry it through town. Whatever excuse they make, it's sure to follow me for some time to come.

VI · Soul Searching

TOM SLIPPED DOWN the tree trunk and landed on the crisp blanket of leaves below. He was still laughing to himself as he sauntered into the woods that bordered the narrow road. As he approached a cluster of hazel trees, he thrust his hand into his pocket and withdrew a neatly folded cloth bag.

With a flap, he unfurled it to its full size, contemplating the fact that it could appear so small, yet hold so much. Never once did he glance behind him or consider the possibility that the constable might have changed his mind and decided to pursue him.

I know the fear in which many of the townspeople hold me, he mused, and I miss my guess if those lawmen don't fit as neatly into that category as this drawstring sack fit into my pocket. 'Tis only necessary to know the technique of folding the bag into the proper shape.

As Tom approached the slender trees, he could see that many of the hazelnuts had ripened, slipped from their leafy encasement upon the branches, and dropped to the ground. There is nature's bounty ready for the taking, Tom thought as he set to gathering handfuls of the yellow-brown nuts and dropping them into his sack.

He worked with purpose, his back bending easily to the task and his thoughts concentrating on ways in which he could preserve and eat the delectable morsels. His thoughts were interrupted by the sound of crackling twigs and the rustling of leaves in the forest. He turned to see an old man, covered from head to toe in a black cloak, bending behind him and dropping nuts into a covered straw basket he had slung over his arm.

47

"Ho, old man," Tom chuckled. "You nearly startled me, you came up so sudden."

"Sudden?" snapped the man. "I've been here long before you. This is my gathering place, and you've no right to take my nuts."

Tom stared at the man in amazement, and the old man glared back. His face was partially covered by the cloak's wide hood, but Tom could see that his face was as wrinkled as an apple doll, and he seemed older and more knotted than the trees themselves.

"Have no fear," Tom said soothingly. "I shall only fill a sackful. There is a bounty of nuts for us both."

"Hrumph," grumped the old man as he turned back to his task. "There are never enough for me." His hand reached out from under the cloak, and gnarled, twisted fingers grasped a fallen hazelnut firmly. With a quick, darting movement that seemed to belie his years, he thrust the nut roughly into his basket and closed the lid tightly.

He seems to think they'll run away if he doesn't close them in, Tom thought with amusement. 'Twill take him a fortnight if he picks them up one at a time like that. What a strange old man.

Tom had never seen the man before, although he believed himself to be acquainted with every person living around Westborough. "Where do you make your home, old man, and what be your name?" he asked in a friendly manner.

"I live where I am welcome," answered the old man in a weak voice, "and I am called by many names. It matters not what people call me, for I enter at their door as soon as I enter their thoughts."

Then the old man fell silent, and Tom began to feel uneasy in his presence. Tom moved farther from the grove, where the hazelnuts were scattered about in plain sight, and hunted for nuts that were hidden in the underbrush and under layers of crackling brown leaves. It will be easier for him to fill his basket with nuts from the clearing, Tom thought, and perhaps he will leave when he has his fill.

The pair worked in silence. Tom bent low over the ground and found nuts under every leaf he turned, while the old man worked slowly and painfully, picking up one nut at a time and shutting the basket lid tightly after each captured nut was dropped in.

Tom could barely believe his success. With every handful of nuts that he tossed into his sack, the contents seemed to swell as though he had dropped in ten times as many. In just a short space of time, his sack was full and he was ready to go on his way.

As he lifted the bulging sack over his shoulder, he glanced back at the old man. His gaunt body was still bent over his task, and his basket sounded emptier with each gathered nut. Tom looked at his own heavy sack and felt pity for the man.

Perhaps I should stay and fill his basket for him, he thought, or offer to trade the empty basket for my full sack. Tom turned and held the bag in front of him. "Here, old man," he offered. "Take these nuts and be on your way. I shall stay and fill the empty basket for myself. 'Tis no trouble."

The old man lifted his face toward Tom, but his back remained bent. He clutched the basket tighter to his body and shook his head slowly. His eyes seemed hollow and possessed a faraway look, as if they did not see Tom at all.

"I have come here to gather my harvest for centuries, it seems, and still I never have enough. Never enough." His voice sounded hard and sad at the same time, and Tom felt a shiver of fear at the old man's strange words. He was anxious to be on his way but felt it was his duty to remain until he had helped the old man in any way he could.

"Let me fill your basket for you then," he offered. "I can do it quickly, and fill it to the brim."

"I believe you can do that," the man decided, "but the nuts here are not what I am looking for. There is a much better gathering spot not far from here where the nuts are plump and round and ripe for the picking. There a basket can be filled quickly. Come, follow me." The old man beckoned to Tom with a crooked finger.

Surely there were other hazel groves, Tom thought with annoyance, but what was wrong with the one in which they were now? He did not wish to waste the day following after the old man, but he had cast his lot and he did not see a polite way out of the bargain. He had offered to help, and the old man needed him.

Obediently, Tom followed the cloaked figure out of the clearing and deeper into the forest. Graceful white birches with yellow leaves gave way to dappled maple trees and then to towering black pines as the silence of the forest enveloped them. Directly west they traveled, the old man moving rapidly through the leaves and bushes, while Tom marveled at his pace.

Every now and then, the bent figure would turn and crook his bony finger to beckon Tom to follow. The woods became dense, and the trees were so tall and thick that Tom could no longer see the sun. Soon the old man entered a part of the forest with which Tom was unfamiliar. Could they be going as far as Upton town?

Then the pair passed along the shores of murky Hobomoc Pond. The Nipmuc Indians had called it Hoccomocco, the name of their great evil spirit. Few ventured near its shores because of the legend of evil that surrounded it. From the center of its waters Tom saw the cairn of stones that marked the site where a beautiful Nipmuc maiden was drowned by her spurned lover.

"Hurry!" demanded the old man, and Tom stopped his reverie and moved to keep up with the beckoning hand of his unwanted guide. Faster and faster went the old man's stride, through thickets and brambles, across deep coverings of pine needles, and up the steepening slope.

Tom was growing weary, and the rope of his nut sack cut into the flesh of his hand. He shifted the bag uneasily and tried to keep up, pushing away the brambles and branches that crossed his path as he walked. "How much farther?" he called, but the old man did not turn.

A short distance ahead, surrounded by craggy rocks and sparsely treed peaks, the wizened figure stopped and pointed to a lush stand of hazels. The richly foliated trees were in sharp contrast with the gloomy surroundings and barren rocks, and Tom was sure he had never seen or heard of this grove before.

Thank goodness we've arrived, he thought, sitting wearily on a gray granite rock. He set his heavy sack down beside him and wondered how the old man had outwalked him, considering Tom's strength.

He looked around at the unfamiliar surroundings. A rocky ledge jutted out of the hillside, and a shallow cave nestled under its protection. Smoldering embers flickered from a circle of stones near the cave entrance.

Could this be where the old man lives? Tom thought incredulously. Why, this is Boston Hill! There's little wonder I've never set my foot on this Godforsaken spot. 'Tis said there are more rattlesnakes and wolves on this hill than there are people in the great city of Boston!

The old man walked past the cave to a neatly stacked pile of logs, dragged two roughly cut pieces to the dying fire, and threw them on. He stoked up the embers with a long stick, and immediately a roaring fire blazed up.

'Tis his home after all, Tom thought in amazement. He

must be one of those queer souls who live alone, away from all the world. But why Boston Hill? I must fulfill my bargain quickly and betake myself home.

Tom called to the old man as he stood at the fire. "Give me the straw basket and I shall fill it forthwith." He walked toward the stand of hazels, and the old man approached slowly, the basket dangling from his arm.

When Tom took the basket in his own hand, he was shocked by its heaviness. How could an empty reed basket weigh so much? The old man drew back to the edge of the clearing and watched Tom as he placed the basket on the ground near the fallen nuts.

This will take no time at all, he consoled himself, and then I shall be on my way. At least I will have done the fellow a good turn.

The nuts were unusually fat and round and their shiny brown shells waited to be gathered. Tom reached out his hand to scoop up a fistful, but the nuts seemed to roll out of his reach just as he closed his hand over them.

This is uncommon strange, he thought fearfully. He looked up to see the old man's hollow eyes staring at him intently. Tom set his sights on one plump nut and placed his hand deliberately and slowly over it. With one quick stroke, he had grasped it in his hand. He lifted the closed lid of the basket and began to drop in his prize, when his eyes focused clearly on the nut in his hand.

It was brown and hard, but it moved of its own free will, and when Tom opened his hand and brought it closer to his face, he saw that the thing had arms and legs and was struggling and squealing in fear.

"Quickly! Drop him into the basket!" the old man yelled.

Tom looked into the straw basket and saw three more tiny creatures running frantically for the open lid. The hair on the back of Tom's neck rose in a shiver of fear. His eyes opened as wide as a gaping knothole, and his stomach turned cold and leaden within him. A scream escaped his lips as he dropped the frightening thing that he had so confidently plucked from the forest floor as an innocent hazelnut.

A cackling laugh resounded through the forest, and Tom turned to gaze at the old man. His toothless mouth was open in a wide grin, and laughter echoed from his thin throat.

Tom moved to run from the forest, but his legs were frozen in fright and he could not make them turn and carry him away. It was like a dream he often had in which a gleaming black snake suddenly uncoiled from the underbrush and moved to strike at him. The nightmare was always the same, and in it, Tom looked in horror at the poised snake, unable to move out of danger.

The wizened man pulled back the black hood and pointed a bony finger at Tom. "You see, 'tis not an easy task gathering souls. They fight and struggle and you must be wily to hold them fast. I need you to help me fill my basket, Tom. 'Tis never full enough!" The old man glared at Tom. White hair flowed back on his head like a wild mane, and his shriveled face seemed lost in its fullness.

"Did you think I had forgotten you, Tom? Forgotten you?" he bellowed. Then his voice changed to a wheedling tone. "I need you, Tom. How pleased I was this morning when you tricked the sheriff. But last night, I writhed in pain to see you deny yourself that pudding. I tried so hard to show you it was rightfully yours. You must indulge yourself more. There is so much I can offer you, if you only let me, Tom. Fine clothes, money in your pockets, and a bounty of food to grace your table every day. You should welcome me into your life, Tom, for your soul is already mine."

"No!" Tom shouted. "No!" The word echoed off the

granite cave and was repeated hollowly throughout the silent forest.

"Yes!" the old man shouted back at him angrily. Then his voice softened again. "You are forgetting how I saved you from the fever so many years ago."

The old man advanced a step toward Tom, as he reached into his cloak and pulled out a rolled parchment scroll. He did not open it but shook it in Tom's direction as he spoke. "I have helped you in the past. I can be with you whenever you need me. I can help you, Tom, but you must help me in return. This pact makes you mine. 'Tis a bargain that I won't forget, Thomas Cook!"

I shall never be swayed by your temptations, Tom thought in defiance, but his voice would not utter a sound. His eyes were riveted on the old man, when suddenly the bent figure vanished, and the cloak collapsed in a bodiless pile and was immediately consumed in flames.

At his feet, the basket also disintegrated in fire, and as Tom looked at it, the forest floor became marked with the charred black pattern of woven straw. A cackling laugh drifted on the wind, and Tom was released. His legs moved as swiftly as those of a frightened deer, and he ran from the hill as though the devil were chasing him.

Tom ran blindly through the forest, leaving his nuts and his wits behind him. Branches whipped at his arms and legs, sweat beaded on his forehead, and his body grew weary from running, but he would not stop. Forward he ran, forward, thinking, I must get home. Home!

The Old Post Road loomed ahead, and Tom pushed his weary body until he reached his cabin. Bursting through the door, he collapsed, sweating and panting, on the dirt floor.

Through the weariness that engulfed his body, Tom looked around his cabin. A roaring fire blazed in the grate and bathed the room in warmth. Perched on the small wooden table was a bushel basket filled with hazelnuts.

Tom was confused. Had he been dreaming, or could this be more of Beelzebub's work? If so, Tom would throw the cursed nuts out.

He struggled to his feet, and as he did so he noticed that a message had been scratched into the dirt floor. Tom sank to his knees and read: "Deer Tom, Here's yer nuts. Yer friend, Jesse."

VII · A Fish Story

TOM SLEPT FITFULLY that night, despite his exhaustion, and his dreams were haunted with visions of the wrinkled old man and the terrified nutsouls. It was nearly morning before he gave up all hope of enjoying a peaceful rest, and when he rose with the gray light of dawn, he ached with a tiredness that filled his body and his mind.

Stepping gingerly across the cold floor, he walked to the fireplace and stared at the glowing embers as if they held an answer to his fears.

I've tried to live by God's word, he thought to himself, helping others and asking nothing for myself. But still, Beelzebub claims my soul, and I have not been able to rid myself of his constant tormenting. I must gather my wits about me and find the answer to his hold upon me, for when the devil shows his withered face again, I must be ready.

A neat stack of cut logs had been placed on the hearth, and Tom was sure he had young Jesse to thank. He pulled two heavy pieces from the pile and threw them onto the grate. As he poked the fading embers and blew half-heartedly into the ashes, smoke curled obligingly from the fresh logs and the fire grew to life as it consumed the weathered wood.

"I've got to think," Tom muttered to himself. He pulled a chair up to the hearth, and as he did so, he glanced upon the message Jesse had left scratched in the floor. He had forgotten about the boy's note, and the recollection of his surprise at finding it the night before floated across his mind like another of his fading dreams.

That Jess is a friend to me as sure as Beelzebub is not, he

mused. The boy looks up to me, I think, and I can't let him down. What would he have thought of me if he had seen me running down Boston Hill like a frightened fawn?

A knock on the door interrupted Tom's thoughts, and he was startled by the intrusion of the sound. "Who is it?" he called gruffly, surprised at his own apprehension.

Jesse's voice answered through the chinks in the door, and Tom opened it to welcome the boy. The sight of his eager face released a knot that had tightened Tom's chest, and he clasped his arms around the boy's slender back.

"I'm powerful glad to see you," Tom said. "You cannot know how the stacked wood and the glowing fire warmed my heart. How did you know I'd be back last night?"

"After Meeting, all the talk was of how the devil helped you escape. The sheriff swears you are bewitched. He says that old Beelzebub himself must have untied your hands and lifted you up from the horse, while he and his deputy could not move a muscle. When they tried to give chase, the sheriff said, the devil's laugh filled the forest."

Tom's prediction that the sheriff would blame the devil for the escape had not been wrong. He smiled grimly to himself. So it was the devil's laugh, was it? If only the sheriff had heard the sound of the devil's laugh, he would never again mistake it for Tom's.

"I didn't believe a word about Beelzebub, and neither did Pa," Jesse went on, "but it was a joy to hear you fooled the sheriff. How did you do it?"

"A boastful man fools himself," Tom replied. "I only had to let the sheriff be himself, and my escape was sure."

Tom settled Jesse on the stool near the fireplace and filled the kettle to brew some tea. "I found your note, Jess, and those nuts were a welcome boon. I had gathered a bagful myself, but Fate fouled my day and I lost the lot of them, sack and all."

Tom's stomach sank at the thought of his encounter with Beelzebub, and he hoped his fear did not show on his face. He did not want to frighten the boy with the tale of what had happened to him in the clearing, but Jesse seemed to sense that the subject of what befell the nuts was closed to discussion and did not pursue it.

"I've come to tell you that Pa's pressing cider today, and he'd be pleased if you'd join in. There's so much harvesting going on that they've even closed the school so all the children can help out at home. Everybody who can lend a hand will carry home a share, Pa says, so you'd be helping us and earning something for yourself, too."

Tom let out a muffled chuckle. "So you thought you'd drag me to a cider pressing, did you? You're getting to be as wily as I am. You know I always work alone. The folks would be startled if I joined in, especially after my run-in with the sheriff yesterday."

"There's only friendly folks coming, Tom, like the Ludlows and the Caxtons. Pa's told them you've been invited to join in, and they accepted his decision."

"Not without an argument, I'd wager," Tom added. "I grant you there are families who don't hold with the claim that I'm in league with Beelzebub, but they don't ask to work by my side, either."

"Pa needs you. There's such a bounty of apples, he fears they'll rot on the trees for lack of picking. You'd do us a good turn if you'd join in, and I believe you'll enjoy working with the folks. 'Tis hard work but full of merriment, and Ma will serve up a chowder for all. Please, Tom."

"You're kind to ask, lad, but I've work to do before winter. There's traps to be made and apples to be dried and wood to be cut—"

"We need you, Tom." Jesse's eyes met Tom's intense gaze and refused to waver.

"You're a rascal!" Tom laughed, tousling Jesse's hair and pulling playfully at his short club-tail. He noted that the bobbing club-tail was a new addition to the boy's grooming, and his hair was just barely long enough to be pulled back. It was tied with a thin leather thong, just like Tom's.

"I'm not even dressed yet," Tom protested, but it was an acceptance of the offer, nonetheless.

"Finish your tea," Jesse ordered; "then I'll tackle the chores while you're dressing."

Tom gulped down his tea and then set to shaving, but each time he looked in the makeshift mirror, he caught the reflection of Jesse working busily about the cabin, straightening Tom's bedcovers and storing the nuts in a cool corner of the cabin, away from the fire's direct heat.

Perhaps 'tis the lad who will be the very means of my salvation, Tom thought. He draws me out and eases me into the life of the town. 'Tis possible that if my mother had only had a friend by her side, she would never have known the hopelessness that drove her to her awful bargain.

Jesse's bustling about the cabin was completed, and he settled back down on the stool while Tom buttoned on his suspenders. "You know why I always sleep in my britches?" he riddled the boy. When he saw Jesse's blank look, he grinned and said, "If you'd been chased as often as I have, you wouldn't have to guess!"

Jesse laughed. "Speaking of your clothes," he said, "them galluses are mighty worn. They don't look like they'll hold up anything but air!"

Tom joined in the joke, laughing and pulling out the ragged suspenders with his thumbs and letting them snap back against his chest. "Why, these galluses hold up my soul! I've buttoned them on nearly every day of my grown life. It would take the devil himself to make me part with these old friends." Tom chuckled, but he knew it was not his suspenders that the devil wanted. If only the solution were that simple! He would surely trade his suspenders to save his soul.

With humor and companionship to bind them together, Tom and Jesse left the cabin and set off down the path to the Baxters' place. Jesse looked forward, he said, to an entire day with no lessons except those he would learn from his father about cider pressing, and the satisfying feeling of picking apples without keeping count on a slate.

Buoyed by the hope that his new friendship with Jesse would be the key to his escape from Beelzebub, Tom drew the willow flute from his pocket, tapped his Bible with a confident pat, and began to pipe a tune to set his heart to dancing. The pair followed the footpath as it wound its way along the banks of Lake Chauncy, listening to the rhythmic lapping of the waves against the shore and watching the sun glinting across the rippling water.

As they approached one sandy clearing, Tom spied James Wharton dozing against a tree trunk, a fishing line tied around his sausage-like toe. Without a word, Tom stopped moving and placed a cautioning hand across Jesse's chest to put him on the alert. He pointed silently to the snoozing fisherman and gestured to his friend to stay where he was.

As silently as a bobcat stalking his prey, Tom moved to the shore and surveyed the scene. Master Wharton had been up early and found the fish biting, it seemed, for a reed basket bulged with the wriggling fish as it rocked gently on the incoming waves.

The fisherman seemed to have expended all his energies reeling in the creatures of the deep, or else he was not accustomed to such an early hour. His back rested against the sappy trunk of a towering pine, his head lolled gracelessly against his chest, and his white wig was twisted askew. Wharton's shoes and stockings had been laid carefully aside, and from his open mouth emanated loud, grunting snores.

Tom's face lit up in a smile as he crept noiselessly back to where Jesse waited. The flute went back to Tom's lips and he began to pipe a merry tune as loudly as he could, hoping to overpower the sound of Wharton's thundering snores.

Opening his eyelids slowly, Wharton was wide awake the moment his eyes focused on Tom, but it was the Leveller who spoke first. "How are the fish biting this fine morning, neighbor?"

James Wharton regarded Tom warily and allowed as how the fish were fairly jumping into his basket. His bushy eyebrows knotted in a frown and seemed to form an unbroken wooly line across his brow.

"Entertaining visitors?" Tom queried in his best New England tone. "You must have enough fish to make a feast for ten starving men."

" 'Tis a day of rest, and I only catch the slimy creatures for the sport," Wharton answered gruffly. "I shall cast all but two of the bloody devils back to the lake when I head home. 'Tis no business of yours, Thomas Cook, and I want no trouble from you!"

"Trouble?" said Tom in mock surprise. He wondered why Wharton did not accuse him of stealing the pudding, but he guessed that after the episode with the sheriff, Wharton was reluctant to remind Tom who was responsible for his arrest. "Young Baxter and I are on our way to help his pa press cider. There's a good deal of apple picking to be done, and every able-bodied soul will lend a hand. If you care to join us, there's a share of cider in it for you." Tom gave Wharton a friendly wink.

The heavy man's face turned red, and he heaved himself up from the sandy beach to face his tormentor squarely. He smoothed the wig and pulled his shirt and waistcoat straight, trying to preserve an image of dignity, but his hairy legs stuck out from beneath his britches, and the fishing line was still tied around his toe, and Tom was nearly driven to gales of laughter.

"I'm no apple picker," Wharton declared angrily, as if Tom had called him a dirty name. "I want no insults from the likes of you, so be on your way and leave me in peace."

"No need to rile yourself, Master Wharton," Tom smiled soothingly. "Enjoy your day of leisure. It sure would be mighty fine to spend a day fishin' in the sun. Mighty fine."

With that, Tom put his flute to his lips and headed down the path playing a merry tune, with Jesse following silently behind. Wharton watched them go and did not settle back to his fishing until the sound of their footsteps could no longer be heard and the notes of the flute had faded into the distant air.

It was just what Tom had expected, for the wily Leveller had not gone off without a second thought about the gentleman's basket of fish. He had walked a short distance from the path, letting his footsteps fall gentler and gentler, and piping his tune softer and softer until he knew Wharton thought him long gone. In point of fact, Tom was just a few feet off, resting on a fallen log with his friend and listening for the heavy snores that soon wafted toward his ears from the direction of the shore.

"Do you favor fried perch?" Tom whispered.

Jesse grinned and gave an enthusiastic nod.

"Do you think Master Wharton ought to dump those wounded fish back into Chauncy without a fightin' chance for survival?"

Jesse grinned again and shook his head in a vigorous no, his club-tail swinging about behind.

From his vest pocket, Tom drew out two small balls of

string. He carefully unraveled them and smoothed out the tangles. He beckoned silently to Jesse, and the pair walked noiselessly back to the beach.

Jesse nervously eyed the sleeping Wharton, but Tom never gave him a thought or a glance. He concentrated on removing the fish from the basket and stringing them through their open gills. Working quickly, Tom finished his task and handed the string of gleaming fish to his friend.

Not content to simply remove the fish and be gone, Tom gave Jesse an impish grin and approached the sleeping Wharton. He owed the farmer something for the inconvenience he had caused Tom the morning before. Cautiously, Tom untied the fishing line from around the gentleman's fat toe and tied it securely to his own piece of string. Taking the free end, he fastened it tightly around the dangling white club-tail of Wharton's beribboned wig. Finally, he placed the center of the long string loosely around the protruding toe.

Satisfied with his work, Tom boldly put his willow flute to his lips while Jesse followed him behind the dense brush that lined the path. Wharton stirred in his sleep, and Jesse joked that his dreams must be filled with sounds of music. It was several minutes before the lively notes awakened Wharton, but Tom reassured Jesse that the show that would surely follow would be worth the wait. He put his flute away as they watched Wharton stretch and stand up just as the fishing bob gave a jerk. Apparently eager to reel in one last fish, he moved to pull in the line.

Before his heavy body could reach down to unfasten the string, however, the fish gave a powerful tug, the line unraveled from around the gentleman's toe, and a startled expression showed on his face. " 'Tis a strange, sliding sensation about his head," Tom whispered knowingly. Before Wharton could gather his wits about him, the wig was pulled from his head and dragged across the beach to the water's edge.

"My wig!" Wharton exclaimed, waddling after it as fast as his chubby legs could carry him. "My wig!" The fish was sleeker and faster than the fisherman, however, and in a moment, Tom, Jesse, and Wharton watched the line, the bob, and the precious wig disappear beneath the water.

Brushing his few matted hairs with his fingers, Wharton tried to discern what had happened. "The wig moved as though it were bewitched," he marveled aloud. Tom knew the thought of replacing the expensive wig irritated Wharton, and he was not surprised to see the color rise in his cheeks as he angrily lifted the dripping reed basket from the cold lake waters. Wharton's surprise was doubled when he found it held nothing but two solitary fish. He rechecked the fastening on the lid and saw no fault with it. Another mysterious disappearance, his expression seemed to say. Wharton looked with confusion from the basket to the path where Tom had disappeared.

"He suspects us," Jesse whispered, "but he saw us leave without touching the basket."

"Thunderation!" muttered the gentleman to himself, while he pulled on his stockings and shoes. " 'Tis true what they say about Tom Cook. The devil's work shows its ugly face again." He snatched up his nearly empty basket and stalked home, looking about nervously, apprehensive that someone might see him unwigged.

"What a tale he'll have to tell about this day of fishing!" Tom giggled under his breath. "He'll tell them all that the wily Tom Cook has charmed the fish from the basket and the wig from his pate without ever laying a hand on them!"

Jesse gleefully finished Tom's sentence for him. "And everyone will believe him!"

VIII · Hard Pressed

AN AIR OF festivity mingled with the sweet smell of ripe apples in Jed Baxter's orchard. When Tom and Jesse arrived bearing their gift of fresh perch, the Baxter and Ludlow children were excitedly racing from one heavily laden tree to the next, filling straw baskets with the juicy fruit.

Joseph Caxton and Noah Ludlow helped Baxter keep the press filled with apples, and all three men shared the task of turning the handle that ground the fruit into pulp, letting the golden juice flow freely into the wooden cask set beneath its spigot.

"Where've you been to?" Prudence Baxter chided her son when the pair arrived. "Pa's been waiting on you, boy!"

"I fear 'tis my fault," Tom apologized politely, presenting the string of fish to Jesse's mother. "We ran across James Wharton at Lake Chauncy and he shared this bounty of perch for all those helping with the cider pressing. He had more fish than he could eat, and if we didn't help ourselves to the bounty, he was fixing to throw these poor devils to the bottom of the lake."

"Well, bless his heart," Goody Baxter said, softening. "I didn't know Master Wharton could be so kind. These fish will be a real complement to the corn chowder I have simmering over the coals. 'Tis turning out to be a real corn dance today. We'll rival the old Nipmucs with our harvest celebration!" She paused a moment and then looked kindly at Tom. "Jed and I are grateful for your help. We want you to know you're welcome here."

Tom stood in embarrassment as Jesse smiled broadly.

"That chowder sure smells good," Tom said, changing the subject, and then headed toward the orchard. I remember Pa and Ma joining their neighbors to raise a barn roof or bale a field of hay, he thought warmly, and a shared meal was always the best part of the day. Things had changed so much for him since those early times.

He recalled his mother saying that feasting and merry-making made the work seem easier and passed the day more quickly. Tom turned to see the good wives working over the noonday meal. As they did, they sang a hymn to express their thanks for the bountiful harvest. Their strong voices carried up the hill to the cider press and floated down over the children as they gathered apples in the orchard.

It was the first time Tom had ventured to help in a cider pressing. In fact, it was the first community effort he had joined at all. He guessed that the significance of the occasion was not lost on Jesse. He probably allows himself no small amount of satisfaction at having convinced me to come, he thought.

Tom eased his way into the orchard, thinking he would pick apples alone, but the children spied him and were not about to leave him a solitary man.

"Oh, 'tis Tom Cook!" they shouted as they saw the slender figure slip amongst the trees. Tom responded with a tousle and a tease for each of the youngsters as they swarmed about him.

"Did you fetch us that grand puddin' t'other night?" asked young Bess Ludlow. "Did you, Tom? I know you did!" Her eyes were wide in admiration of her mysterious benefactor, and her pigtails, tied up in bright strips of cloth, bobbed up and down as she hugged Tom's legs.

Tom only laughed, scaled an apple tree like a squirrel, and began shaking the branches until the rosy fruit fell like rain around the squealing children below.

"If I ever set my hands on a whole puddin," Tom called, "I'd eat it afore anyone could claim it for his own!"

Secretly, he hoped the children knew better than to believe his prattle, for he rarely kept a thing for himself and always distributed his booty to those in need.

"Tom!" Jesse called as he descended the hill. "Ho, Tom! Pa asks if you'd be so kind as to take a turn at the press. The men up there say their arms are plain wore out. I'll help the younguns with the apple picking. 'Tis truly more fun than work, don't you think?"

Tom was secretly amused at Jesse's grown-up attitude. He's determined to keep me in the mainstream of activity, he thought. He's really just a youngun himself; yet he seems certain that I'll fit right in to this community effort once I try it. Tom slid down the tree trunk obligingly and tossed a handful of apples into a nearly full basket. Hoisting the heaping container up onto one shoulder, he let out an exaggerated grunt.

"You call this fun? I'm already wore out, for 'tis more work than a lazy man like myself can bear. I'll never survive the whole day, Jess."

The boy laughed at Tom's mock complaints and watched as Tom made his way up the slope to the edge of the orchard, whistling to the tune of the women's hymn.

As he neared the wooden press, Tom saw that the Reverend Ebenezer Parkman had come to wish the Baxters godspeed with the work and perhaps offer a prayer or two in time for the noonday meal. Tom was disappointed to see the reverend there, for the two men never could seem to greet each other without ending up in an argument.

The Reverend Mr. Parkman stood solemnly, his white wig and ministerial bands adding to his air of authority. That man has been the sole religious leader of Westborough since before I first opened my eyes to the world, Tom thought, and his power over everyone in town would be complete if it weren't for me and my "evil ways."

A surprised look stole across the minister's face as he saw Tom among the helpers. "Bless me if it isn't Thomas Cook!" he exclaimed. "What brings you out today, son?"

"Son?" Tom echoed. "I'm nobody's son but my mother's, and I'm here to help my neighbor. 'Tis that simple."

"Bless me," the reverend repeated in astonishment, and his pleasure was evident. "I hope you are joining the fold, Thomas, and leaving the devil's ways to follow with God. I've prayed for your salvation and striven with your soul since you were a babe. 'Tis a big step forward to see you amongst the flock of worshipers."

"Ain't no one follows God more than Tom Cook," countered the young man with a tone of defiance. It was an argument that had gone on for many years. Parkman wanted Tom to confess his "thieving ways" before the congregation and become a regular church-goer, but Tom believed that he had to carry out the message of the Bible in the ways that suited his solitary life.

"You must give up your thieving ways, Thomas. The Lord commands that you shall not covet thy neighbor's goods." Parkman closed his eyes and gestured pointedly toward heaven, as if praying for assistance in showing Tom the light.

"I carry out the Lord's commandment as well as yourself, Reverend, for the Good Book tells us to love our neighbor and help the needy. I don't tell you how to live, with your fancy house full of glass windows, and your silk stockings and velvet britches, so why should you try to tell me how to live in God's grace?"

Reverend Parkman did not say a single word in response to Tom's outburst, but his teeth clenched tightly and his jaws pulsated silently at the sides of his face. He placed his thumb and forefinger across his temples and closed his eyes, as if summoning the strength to deal with Tom's blasphemous words. Softly, he said, "I give you what admonition, instruction, and caution I can. I beseech God to give it force!"

"I beseech God you leave me in peace!" Tom shouted as he dumped his load of apples into the press and set to turning the crank with fervor. He saw the other men exchange nervous glances. Now I've ruined my chances to be welcomed among the farmers, he thought. No one fights with the reverend, but I can't abide the man! His anger at Parkman's denigration of his life was converted into strength, and he turned the press handle with energy, his face set in a hard look.

Jesse trudged up to the press with another basket of apples just in time to overhear the last few heated words between Tom and Parkman. He set down the basket of apples between Tom and his father, who was trying unconvincingly to act as though the argument had never taken place. The silence over the group was uncomfortable.

Jesse looked at the apples he had carted up. Most of the fruit was overripe, some of the apples were bruised, and more than a few looked as though they had made a feast for worms. "Don't you want to throw out the bad apples, Pa? Look, Tom, some of these here are wormy, 'tis sure." Tom knew that Jesse was trying to calm him down so that he would not leave in anger.

Joseph Caxton seized the opportunity to lighten the tense atmosphere and forced a laugh. His burly arms lifted the basket and poured its entire contents into the press without so much as a glance at their condition. "All those critters liven up the flavor, boy," he chuckled.

Noah Ludlow joined in the joke. "After this here cider

sets a mite and starts to ferment just so, ain't a self-respectin' worm around that would dare to touch a drop!''

The men laughed heartily, but Tom continued to crank with all his might, and he did not feel any humor in the moment. Reverend Parkman stood silently, as if exhausted from his words of advice, and his eyes remained closed introspectively upon his inner self.

Suddenly a dull thudding sound emanated from the press and the crank jammed tightly. Tom's turning jolted to a halt with the handle at the top of its interrupted cycle.

"Thunderation!" he muttered, a mild epithet controlled by the presence of the reverend and the children. "The younguns must have scooped up a stone with the apples.''

Baxter reached down to the ground for a sturdy stick. Parkman approached the press to see what the problem was and offer a prayer for its speedy resolution. He then stood back, carefully folding his hands behind him and eying Tom with a look of smug satisfaction at his ill luck.

Baxter dug the stick down into the core of the press, trying to dislodge the stone, but it could not be located. " 'Tis no use," he said. " 'Tis too far under the shaft. We'll have to take the press apart.''

The group was disheartened by the thought of interrupting the work for the time-consuming and tedious task of dismantling and then reassembling the machine, all for the sake of one small stone.

Tom's anger mounted when he saw the reverend's disdainful look. "No need to take it apart," he offered resolutely. "Maybe I can reach it with my hand. Jed, if you push the crank backwards, we can loosen it up.''

"No," Caxton said, "there's too much danger. We either keep working at it with the stick or take the whole thing apart.''

"Thunderation!" Tom shouted. "Just grab that crank and turn it backward. Time's awastin' with all this talk!"

"Have a caution!" Caxton objected, but Tom had already thrust his hand into the bowels of the press and had convinced Jed Baxter to keep pushing at the handle in a counter motion.

Jed pushed at the jammed handle and Tom groped around until he had worked his fingers under the shaft and laid hold of the stone. "There's the little devil!" he exulted, stealing a glance at the reverend's face.

His joy did not last a moment. No sooner did he pull at the jammed stone, than the crank released itself with pent-up power and the anxious group heard the bone-crushing sound of the shaft as it gripped Tom's fingers within its tight grasp.

Tom's face turned white with pain, and he looked searchingly at the men around him. "My fingers!" he whispered. "The bewitched thing's crushed my fingers."

Immediately, the men set to dismantling the cider press. Wooden pegs and rusty nails were hammered apart while Reverend Parkman held Tom's free hand and offered soothing words. Tom slumped weakly across the barrel of the press, and sweat beaded up on his forehead.

"Don't fear, Tom," Jesse consoled, but Tom could hear the boy's voice trembling. "Ye'll be all right. I'll fetch Doc Horton straightaway."

"No doctoring needed, Jesse," Tom said with false confidence. " 'Tis my cross, and I must bear it like a man. The fingers must heal themselves as they will."

With the creaking sound of wet wood upon tightly knit joints, the cider press loosened and finally released its victim. Tom's hand was gently pulled from the press's grip, and the stone, smaller than the trouble it had caused, fell unnoticed to the grass.

Tom lay down on the soft earth, his fingers limp. "Please let me fetch Doc," Jesse begged, but Tom would not hear of it. He bore a secret resentment of the esteemed Dr. Horton simply because he lived in the home that had once belonged to Tom's family. This deep-seated anger, combined with the prevalent belief that all physical illnesses were God's will, led Tom to shun the doctor and his medicines at all cost.

Faith Caxton and Kate Ludlow had been alerted to the accident, and Tom saw them running up from the cabin with bits of kindling and strips of old sheeting. Little Bess followed worriedly behind her mother, her braids bouncing up and down at every step, a bucket of cold water clutched in her hands.

The women bathed Tom's forehead with cool water while Caxton bound the broken bones tightly against the kindling splints with wide strips of cloth. It was all that could be done at the moment, and Tom would have no more.

Jesse wrung his hands and fought back tears to see his friend suffer. Tom winced and swore under his breath. Reverend Parkman closed his eyes and prayed for Tom's tormented soul.

"I fear 'tis the wrath of God visiting you for your sins, Thomas Cook," he intoned solemnly. "You must repent and embrace God's ways."

"No!" Tom screamed, startling everyone. " 'Tis Beelzebub upon me again, punishing me for daring to help a neighbor. Curse you, Beelzebub! You'll never get me! Never!"

IX · Remedies

THE REVEREND MR. PARKMAN was the only man to be spared to see to it that Tom arrived home without further mishap. All those who were younger and stronger, including Jesse, were needed more than ever to put the cider press back into operation and to finish the work before nightfall.

The dour, self-righteous minister was not the sort of companion Tom would have chosen for the journey home, but he did possess a fine horse. Tom concluded that riding double with the reverend was preferable to walking the distance alone.

Mercifully, the reverend remained silent, choosing not to continue the argument that had begun earlier. Tom noted this concession with gratitude, for he was in too much agony to waste words arguing.

Perhaps 'tis out of no concern for me that he keeps quiet, Tom thought, but that he mourns for the lost meal. Everyone knows that the proud reverend is beginning to come on the town more and more, what with the price of firewood rising like smoke on a windy day and the price of fine clothes wearing many a man's shirt thin.

Tom had to admit that he had looked forward to the feast at the Baxters' himself, but his mind wandered and he could not dwell on thoughts of perch and chowder long. His fingers swelled, bursting at the splints and bindings, and his entire body coursed with pain.

Parkman helped Tom into his bed and eased off his boots. Taking a dipper of water from the barrel, he offered Tom a drink as gently as one would treat an injured child.

"Rest yourself, Thomas," he said kindly, and he moved to stoke up the fire.

Tom felt the minister's kindness to him, and without the energy needed to combat the older man's views, he felt his opinions softening. He was too tired to think, and his eyes closed into sleep just as he began wondering if there were not some common ground between him and the minister after all.

When Tom opened his eyes again, the day had faded, and it was Jesse Baxter, and not Parkman, who met his gaze.

" 'Tis night," Jesse said softly. "Ma sent me to sleep here and care for you. She says you must soak your hand in the coldest water you can bear. 'Twill lessen the swellin'."

Tom sat up slowly and examined his hand while the boy filled a bucket of water from the barrel outside.

"All broke," he said matter-of-factly when the lad returned. "Every finger busted, includin' the thumb. What a cursed ending to a day that started out so fine."

Tom's fingers were purple from the bruises and the tightness of the splints, but he knew that to remove the bindings would only make things worse. Whatever way the twisted bones set now was the way they would have to knit, for good or ill.

Tom plunged his hand down into the icy water and cringed with the sudden, sharp pain. His head felt light and feverish, and he would have sunk back in agony if the boy had not been there. He looked at Jesse and tried to force a smile. "It ain't bad," he lied.

"Ye don't have to put on for me, Tom. I know how bad you feel. I busted just one finger once, and thought I'd about die!"

Jesse held up the pointer finger of his right hand. It came straight up and then leaned curiously to the left, just above the first knuckle. "And a doctor set this one," he laughed.

Tom took one look at the crooked finger and let out a chuckle in spite of his pain. "So that's what I would have been in for."

"When the doc saw how it healed, he wanted to crack it with a hammer and try again. I wouldn't have none of it. I kept my hands in my pockets whenever he was around!"

"Sometimes those doctors with all their medicines don't show a shred of common sense. I don't put a bit of faith in them. Did you ever hear the story of the farmer out Northborough way? He lived in a meadow by a clear, pure spring. The water kept the cattle fed and grew the crops and served the family's needs every day. The farmer said it was the purest spring that ever ran, and he set great store by it.

"Then one day the farmer took ill. 'Tis the typhoid, decides the old doc, and a real bad case. He tells the farmer and his family that the cause of the fever is the spring and neither the patient, the family, nor the animals is to have a drop.

" 'Twas hard to tell if the farmer was feelin' the blow of his illness more than he was feelin' the loss of that clear-running spring, but each day he grew weaker and the fever grew stronger. Each day he'd ask for a sip of the spring water to wet his lips and cool his brow, but the doc would not yield. 'No water,' he'd say, 'or it'll be the death of him.'

"Finally, the end drew near. The doc left the deathbed to make another call and said he'd return in the evening to prepare the body. With his dying breath the farmer begged his wife for one last drink of water from his precious spring.

"Obliging her husband's last wish, the wife gave the farmer a draught of cooling water. Within the hour, the fever broke, and when the doc returned he found the patient, not dead at all, but sitting up in bed drinking another dipper of water. 'Why, I knew it all the time,' the doc proclaims.

'Fresh, cool water be the cure. Bring more water for the patient and he will be on the road to recovery.' ''

Jesse slapped his knee. "Hah! 'Tis just like the old docs. Find your own cure and they take the credit for it. They have many a strange cure to offer, too. One time Pa had the itches something fierce. 'Twas something he picked up while clearing a field for planting. He called on the doctor, and the doc gives him a receipt. It says wash a whole quart of fishworms clean and stew them up with a pound of hog's lard. Filter the worms through a strainer and mix in half a pint of oil turpentine and half a pint of good brandy. Then you cook the mixture well, let it cool down, and pour it over the itches. Pa rubbed the foul stuff everywhere, but he still nearly scratched himself to death!''

"The only good remedy in that concoction is to take the half-pint of good brandy and pour it down your throat!" Tom laughed. "That is the guarantee for curing the itches and saving a doctor's fee to boot!''

Jesse joined Tom in a hearty laugh, but Tom's smile quickly faded and he looked soberly at the boy. "Why'd you come, Jess? What makes you hang around me so?''

"I admire you, Tom. Don't you know that? I want to be your friend. I want to be like you and learn to use my wits to help others.''

"Well, you've started your helping with the right man, Jess. I've needed a friend and didn't know how to make one.'' Tom glanced down at his swollen hand and thought that perhaps he had thwarted Beelzebub again, for he had lost his battle with the cider press but gained a closeness to Jesse that he had not had before.

Tom and Jesse talked long into the night, and when the boy's eyes began to close, Tom set the bucket down and bade his friend get some sleep. With his sound right hand, Tom undid his suspenders, and Jesse knew exactly where to hang them. Then Tom crept under the covers and Jesse crawled in between two blankets laid out before the fire, and the two slept.

It was weeks before Tom was able to move his injured hand at all, and during this time he kept close to the cabin. Jesse stayed on from the first night, and soon he seemed to Tom to be an indispensable part of the household.

Each morning they shared tea and tidied the cabin, with Jesse helping Tom to shave and tie back his club-tail. Then the boy set off for school, completed a few chores at his father's farm in the afternoon, and returned to Tom's cabin at the end of the day.

In return, Tom showed Jesse how few vegetables were really needed for a tasty stew, taught him what the forest had to offer the hungry settler, and instructed the boy in how to prepare his own meals. Jesse built a drying rack under Tom's direction, and apples were sliced and dried in the few remaining sunny afternoons and stored away for winter eating.

In the evenings, the pair sat before the fire preparing animal traps to catch rabbits and muskrats for winter meat and sharing stories about the town and the way they had heard things used to be. Sometimes Tom read to Jesse from the Bible, and other times Jesse read aloud from his schoolbooks.

Visitors became more common at the cabin, and it seemed to Tom that having Jesse around made him less fearsome to his neighbors, and more human.

The Baxters came to the cabin regularly, and Tom came to know them well. The were kindly people, straightforward in their talk and their actions. Tom finally understood why Jesse had first approached him, ready to judge Tom by his actions and not by rumors and tales, for his openness mirrored that of his parents.

The Baxters sent over jugs of cider and a basket of apples,

although Tom protested that he had not earned a share of the crop, since his stubbornness had caused so much trouble. But Jesse's family would allow no protests and continued to check on Tom's progress and bring soups and loaves of bread for Tom and Jesse to share.

The Caxtons also began stopping by now and then, and the Ludlows sent a few eggs, which Tom savored. He had never seen such sympathy or enjoyed such favors, and he believed he had Jesse to thank for his change of fortune.

It was October now, and Tom knew that his fingers were nearly healed. When Jesse was at school, he secretly tried moving them, and he occasionally tried picking up things with his fingertips. He felt it was time to remove the splints but prolonged the inevitable moment, knowing that as soon as he could fend for himself again, Jesse would have to return to his family's farm. The Baxters had generously spared him for too long already.

Tom began to doubt his own goals and often debated with himself during the quiet moments he spent alone. I've got to set out on the road again and be of some use to my neighbors, he would think. Then his thoughts would be countered with arguments against taking any more risks. 'Tis true I broke my fingers while helping out, and I can't take chances any more. Who would help me if I were injured again?

One evening, as Tom and Jesse prepared for bed, the boy goaded Tom into planning an adventure.

"I won't be here much longer, Tom. Pa says your fingers should be about healed. I've learned a lot from you about trapping and cooking, but 'tis rather dull hanging about the cabin so much. Let's walk up toward the Stones' house tomorrow and see if we can find some excitement. What do you say, Tom?"

"I've decided there will be no more adventures for me, Jess. You've given me a chance to change my ways, and that's exactly what I'm fixing to do. I was thinking to head up to Wharton's farm tomorrow and apologize for all I've done and offer to work an honest day for a fair wage."

Jesse's face fell. He looked searchingly at Tom, wondering if this were another of the young man's jokes, but Tom assured him he meant every word of it.

"I know you're still feeling poorly, Tom," the boy argued, "but when your fingers are healed, you'll feel differently. Folks depend on you, Tom."

"Not for the right things, though. My fingers are as healed as they'll ever be." With no excuses left to offer, Tom pulled at the soiled strips of sheeting and removed the splints that had tried to bind his fingers straight.

He held his hand in front of him and gingerly flexed it. While his fingers resembled the gnarled roots of an ancient oak, he could move each one in its own way, and he was grateful for regaining some use of his hand.

The next day, Jesse returned to his home, and from then on, Tom only imagined the boy's figure bent over his books of an evening, with the firelight flickering across his contented face.

X · Grain Lift

TOM HAD LESS than a week in which to miss having Jesse as a constant companion, for as Saturday dawned, the boy was at his cabin begging for a chance to participate in one of Tom's escapades.

"So, 'tis adventure you seek, is it?" Tom teased. "Don't you know 'tis the adventures that find me, and not t'other way about?"

"You must have plans, Tom, for you've helped not a soul since you busted your fingers in Pa's press. Don't you just itch to be out on the road?"

Tom held up his twisted fingers, examining the knotted bones. He no longer felt the spark of boldness that always seemed to drive him off on another adventure.

"I can't risk another accident like this one, Jess," Tom said flatly. "Perhaps Reverend Parkman was right, for once, and God is sending me a message."

"But your fingers were broke when you were helping us, Tom," Jesse argued. " 'Tis Beelzebub tormenting you again."

"Maybe," Tom said, "but I think I'll stick more to home now that winter is coming on."

"You sound like an old man huddled by the fire," Jesse baited him.

"Whether that is true or not," Tom retorted, "you know well enough that arguing will not change my mind."

Jesse looked downcast. He settled on the stool near the fire and scratched letters idly into the dirt floor. "Pa said over supper last night he expects Goody Rowles will come to Meetin' Sunday and ask for the church's help. Ma says her good-for-nothing husband up and left without a word, and she's got the two younguns to care for. The whole town's talking of it, but Pa says there's little sympathy.''

Tom mulled over Jesse's piece of news. Reverend Parkman would surely gather the church's members to offer some aid to the woman, but it hurt Tom to think how Priscilla Rowles would have to publicly air her fate and beg for the mercy of her more fortunate neighbors. He felt strongly that her supplication showed a lack of pride and independence, but he understood how helpless she must feel with the sudden desertion of her husband.

"Goin' to Meeting, is she?" Tom said bitterly. " 'Tis a manner designed to humiliate. Being a woman, Goody Rowles will not even be allowed to speak for herself. She'll have to stand under the congregation's stern gaze while Reverend Parkman pleads her cause."

"I know," Jesse said. "Pa says each man will write his gift upon a ballot, and the deacons will collect the slips and present them to the minister. 'Tis only he who can know what has been pledged. At least Goody Rowles will get the help she needs."

"For all her shame in approaching the Meeting, the members will pledge precious little," Tom predicted. "There's nothing but contempt for families who come on the town. You know, that congregation has been known to turn families away from the town's borders if they come to settle without any means of support."

"If we can provide some comfort and provision for Goody Rowles," Jesse suggested, "perhaps we can show her that there are those who will help willingly without having to beg from the likes of those at Meetin'."

Tom cleared the teapot and his mug from the table without a word. He knew the boy was trying to jolt him into action. When he did not take up the challenge, he saw the youngster look at him with disappointment.

"I think I'll take a walk up to the mill to see if there's any work needing doing," Tom said to Jesse. "You're welcome to tag along if you don't get in the way."

Jesse followed Tom silently out the door, and they walked through the woods and around the lake. The air was cool and crisp and blew at them from across the water. Tom skirted the road until he had passed the center of town and then walked up the Old Post Road toward the mill. He noted that the traffic on the road increased as they got closer to the mill's creaking wheel.

" 'Tis truly harvest time when the mill is so busy," Tom commented. "I remember times when the miller has run out of sacks." Townspeople passed the pair, carrying one or two bags of freshly ground flour, and a few led farm horses laden with three or four bags.

The sound of a clattering wagon coming down the road reached Tom's ears, and he suddenly leaped from the path and hid behind a raspberry thicket. Jesse did not wait to be told what to do but darted behind the prickly bushes with his companion.

As the pair peered cautiously between the branches, the rotund figure of James Wharton came into view, a new white wig shining like a beacon and his beribboned club-tail swinging from side to side with the bouncing of the wagon. Wharton was driving a wagonload of flour sacks, pulled by a sleek bay mare.

As the wagon rattled by, a gleam of delight shone in Tom's eyes. He leaned over and whispered to Jesse, "Why, 'tis that pork-bellied Wharton with a whole wagonload of flour. Have you ever seen the like? My fingers may be in sorry shape, but I promise you my wits are as sharp as ever.

Do you think Goody Rowles could make do with such a huge sack of flour?''

"She surely would have enough bread for the winter," Jesse agreed, and Tom sensed that the youngster was trying not to let his excitement show. As soon as the wagon passed their hiding place, Tom fell into step behind it, with Jesse at his side. Huge sacks of freshly ground flour loaded down the wagon, and the strong bay walked with effort.

Moving lightly to the back of the wagon, Tom slid one heavy burlap sack onto his shoulder. At first, the suddenness of its weight nearly staggered him, but he quickly regained his stride and walked deftly around the wagon, balancing the sack as if it were lighter than Goody Stone's downy comforter.

Walking up toward the driver's seat, Tom hailed James Wharton like a long-lost friend. "Bless me if it ain't the world's best fisherman," he baited the gentleman.

Wharton turned his head to see Tom Cook walking beside his wagon. His face reddened when he recalled the strange disappearance of the fish, and he smoothed back his wig for reassurance. "You skunk-bellied thief!" he shouted. "I'd swear on a Bible you stole my fish, and I'd wager all I own if you didn't steal my pudding right from my pot some weeks past. You belong in jail, you do, and you'd be there if it weren't for that cowardly sheriff!''

"Now, now, Wharton, let the past be forgotten. I'm nothing but a helpless cripple these days," Tom said, dangling his knotted hand in front of his prey. "Levellin' days are over when a man can't even tie his club-tail back!''

Wharton eyed Jesse suspiciously. "You ought to mind the company you keep, boy, or you'll come to no good," he cautioned sternly.

" 'Tis only that Tom is weakened by his accident," Jesse

replied politely. "A body must help whenever he can, don't you agree?"

Wharton regarded the pair nervously for a moment and then snapped the reins, urging the straining horse to move along faster. The mare pulled harder, but Tom kept pace with the wagon with ease.

"This sack of flour is a mighty hard burden for a cripple," Tom complained, "and I can't ask the youngster to shoulder such a heavy load. I see you've just left the mill yourself. Looks like there was a bountiful harvest of grain for the Whartons this season."

Tom shifted the weight of the sack and let out a grunt as it rested against his shoulder again. "I'm bringin' this flour to Goody Rowles. Her husband up and left the young lass with the two wee ones to care for. I figure this flour will get her through the winter with at least bread for their hungry mouths. Don't you agree the townsfolk should come to her aid?"

"Priscilla Rowles' problems are no affair of mine, and no responsibility, either," Wharton retorted.

"Do you think you could at least find a place for the flour on your wagon? I can walk alongside you till we come near her cabin."

"Get out of my road, you thieving skunk!" Wharton roared. "There isn't a bit of space left on the wagon for another sack, and the horse won't pull no more."

"I venture to say, sir," Tom objected, "that there is but one space left, just the size of a sack of flour, where this load would fit right in. You'd never know the difference if you let me drop it on."

"Begone, I say!" bellowed Wharton. "And the devil take me if I ever carry that sack of flour!"

"I'll be off, then, sir," Tom said smartly, "and offer you the sack no more." Tom and Jesse then slowed their pace, while Wharton picked up his as best he could, and the wagon, minus one sack of flour, lumbered on ahead.

Tom tossed the sack of flour to the side of the road and sat down on it as if it were a big burlap pillow.

"Why are you stopping?" Jesse asked, looking at Tom comfortably watching the traffic pass by.

"I think it would be wise to give Wharton his lead," Tom explained. "It may even happen that we can catch up with him outside of town and relieve him of another bag of flour. The man must have thirty sacks of flour on that wagon; yet he'd rather feed it to the mice than share it with his neighbors."

Jesse stood pacing around Tom, waiting impatiently until his mentor decided it was time to move on. The traffic thinned to an occasional passerby, and Tom knew that there would be a lull in business until afternoon.

"Come along, now," he chided suddenly, in mock annoyance. "You're holding me up."

Jesse said nothing but followed questioningly behind Tom as the young man shouldered the sack of flour and proceeded down the road.

After the pair had walked about a mile, a curious sight met their eyes. Wharton's wagon, laden with flour sacks, was pulled off to the side of the road. The bay mare nibbled at the dry grass at her feet, and her owner was nowhere to be seen.

Tom approached the wagon slowly, looking about for signs of Wharton. He stroked the mare's nose with his crooked fingers, talking to her in soft tones while he surveyed the situation.

"Gone and left you all alone, has he, girl?" he crooned to the docile horse. "Oh, I see, now. He's run the front wheel right into a rut. 'Tis too heavy a load to pull out of there, isn't it? And too much of a problem for Wharton to handle.''

Tom dropped the sack of flour he had been carrying and began pulling the sacks still on the wagon and dropping them onto the road beside it.

"Come on, Jess, lend a hand here, time's awastin'. Still, I'm mighty glad you made me stop and rest a while back."

"I didn't make you stop—" Jesse protested, but Tom interrupted him and continued.

"For now, as you can see, a true adventure has come our way. Lend a hand!"

Tom and Jesse pulled sacks of flour from the back of the wagon as fast as they could, sliding them down and letting them drop behind.

"What are you going to do?" Jesse asked. "What if Wharton comes back?"

"If Wharton has managed to walk home by now, he won't do a thing until he has eaten his noonday meal and ordered his hired hands back for this wagon," Tom said with certainty. "If the mare couldn't pull it out of the ditch all loaded up, then you're talking about too much work for Wharton to handle alone. I think we'll just pull this wagon back onto the road and deliver the goods to Wharton ourselves. Of course, he'll owe us something for our trouble."

With the load lightened, Jesse climbed up on the seat and gave the reins a slap, while Tom pushed the wagon from behind. With a creak and a groan, the wagon wheel jumped the rut and the wagon sat squarely on the road bed.

"Load her up," Tom called, and with Jesse's help, each sack of flour was lifted by its corners and heaved back onto the wagon with its mates. Tom jumped onto the seat, with Jesse beside him, and gave the boy a friendly slap on the back.

"Good work, my friend. Now it's off to Goody Rowles's

to deliver our pay for this hard work. Then it's off to the Ludlows', the Caxtons', and on to a few other families I figure can make use of this bounty."

Jesse laughed at Tom's plan. "Wouldn't Wharton be surprised to see how easily we pulled the wagon from the rut? It wasn't much effort at all."

Tom pulled up at Priscilla Rowles's cabin and gave a loud "Halloo!" Not a sound answered him, and Tom feared that Priscilla had already gone to town to plead her case with Reverend Parkman.

'Tis no matter now, he consoled himself. In fact, 'tis just as well, for she will think this provision comes from a member of the congregation who willingly gives her aid.

Up and down the pathways went Tom and Jesse, dropping off a sack of flour on the doorsteps of remote cabins and dusty farms. Tom would whistle as they approached and holler "One to a customer!" and drive off as quickly as he had come.

As each sack was removed, the mare traveled more easily, and by the time Tom pulled the wagon up to Wharton's door, the horse was stepping lively. At the sound of the creaking wagon lumbering up to his house, Wharton came bursting through the door.

"What are you doing with my wagon!" he yelled at Tom and Jesse.

"Afternoon, Master Wharton," Tom said to the redfaced farmer. "Jesse and I found your wagon stuck on the road from the mill and managed to pull it free. 'Twas backbreaking work, for sure, but we knew it would please you."

"Please me? Please me?" sputtered Wharton. "Why, half the load is gone! You've stolen my flour!"

"Stolen, is it?" said Tom in mock astonishment. He looked at the load behind him and shook his head in disbelief. "Imagine thieves and highwaymen right on the Old

Post Road. 'Tis shocking! Aren't you thankful we came along when we did, or you'd have nary a bag left at all.''

Wharton was too angry to form words. He stood at his door, looking from Tom to the wagon and back again to Tom.

"I know," Tom put in, "you're too grateful to speak. 'Tis nothing, really—don't mention it." His voice trailed off as he sauntered down the road toward town, leaving Wharton in exasperation with his half load of flour.

XI · Jailbait

TOM WAS NOT surprised when the sheriff came to arrest him as he walked through town later that afternoon.

"Stand your ground, Thomas Cook," ordered the sheriff. "I've come to arrest you for the theft of ten sacks of flour from James Wharton. This time you'll not escape me."

"What an ungrateful man! I did not steal Wharton's flour, Sheriff, but merely rescued his wagon and returned it to him." Tom guessed that the fact that Wharton had played the fool while Tom toyed with him vexed the farmer more than the stolen pudding, the disappearing fish, and the lost wig.

"You've done all the thievin' and deviltry you'll ever do, Thomas Cook," intoned the sheriff, and he marched his prisoner into a drafty cell and locked the door securely. "Just as surely as a farmer shoots a skunk for stealing eggs, 'tis certain that this time you'll be hanged for your deeds till you be dead, dead, dead!"

Tom burst out into a surprised laugh. "Wharton hasn't a shred of proof. Would I have brought his wagon back to him if I had stolen his flour? I'm sorry to disappoint you, Sheriff, but if I am sentenced to hang till I be dead, dead, dead, then I will not be there on that day, day, day!"

Out of fear of Tom's revenge or an unwillingness to pronounce such a severe sentence, Doc Horton, who served as the town's justice of the peace, refused to hear Wharton's case against Tom. Several days passed quietly while the lawmen debated the safest method of transporting the prisoner to Worcester for the next session of the Court of Common Pleas.

All the while, Tom was confined within his cell, planning his escape. I'll have to make my plans carefully, he decided, for if I fail, there will be no second chance.

No visitors were allowed to see the accused thief, but Tom was accustomed to being alone, and each day the faithful Jesse would slip unnoticed to Tom's cell window and pass his friend a cheering note. Tom found that the messages were the high point of his day, and he saved them carefully in his pocket, rereading them in the long and quiet hours of evening.

Both the sheriff and his deputy treated Tom with circumspect caution. Their previous experience with this prisoner's unpredictable ways had made them alert to any tricks he might invent. Like the proverbial moth, Tom decided that the pair of lawmen had learned that if they strayed too close to the flame, they would not live to tell of its ever-present danger.

Tom was fed a simple breakfast and a hearty dinner each day, and it was more than he had enjoyed in his own cabin. The sheriff's wife prepared all the food herself, and Tom thought that perhaps the sheriff had been entitled to some bragging, for the fare was always praiseworthy.

Each evening when the tray of victuals arrived, the sheriff insisted that Tom step back to the farthest wall with his back to the cell door and his hands placed clearly upon the wall. Then the sheriff unlocked the cell door and opened it slightly, while the deputy quickly slid the tray across the floor.

Tom was not allowed to drop his hands to turn to face the sheriff until he heard the cell door slam and the lock turn soundly in the keyhole.

There was little pleasure during those slow days of imprisonment, and Tom spent hours playing his flute, reading his Bible, and watching the birds fly south for the winter. The call of the birds as they glided overhead reminded Tom that if he weren't hanged first, he would need more adequate provisions to survive the winter.

He thought of the few fruits and nuts he had put by, and he hoped his animal traps would yield a steady supply of meat. The thought of dried apples made his mouth water, but he did not think he would ever again have an appetite for nuts. Tom shivered at the thought of them. Watching the suffering souls owed to the devil had poisoned Tom's mind against touching another hazelnut, let alone eating one.

He ruminated on his frightening encounter with Beelzebub and on the weave of the basket that burned its imprint into the earth. There were those who said the devil could leave the print of his cloven hooves burned into the ground where he might stand. Many folks in town had walked to Upton to view a strange mark burnished into a fieldstone that was thought to be proof of the tale. The rock jutted out of a pasture, and in its granite a black mark, not unlike a hoofprint, was firmly etched.

Tom played a melancholy tune on his willow flute and thought about his unwitting conflict with Beelzebub. The devil's invisible hand had made many shun him. Still, he had used the story of the Devil's claim upon him to his own advantage more than once. Both the sheriff and the deputy believed in Tom's evil and feared him. Perhaps, Tom thought, that fear will again be my road to safety.

That evening when the supper tray was brought, Tom politely asked the sheriff if he would be so kind as to allow his prisoner a pipeful of tobacco and the chance to enjoy a relaxing smoke.

"A pipeful of tobacco, is it?" asked the sheriff suspiciously. "I've never known you to smoke before."

" 'Tis rare that I can afford the luxury of a sweet-smelling pipe, Sheriff," Tom rejoined. "I can't pay you for the trouble of providing me with such now, but can you deny a condemned man such a simple request? Can you, Sheriff?"

"I'll think on it," said the sheriff, and he left.

Tom smiled to himself. He was sure the sheriff had fallen for the bait, although he did not know how he would force himself to smoke an entire pipeful of tobacco. It was a habit he despised, and the smell of it nearly churned his stomach. Still, it was a sacrifice he would have to make in order to save his neck. His slender neck was a part of his body that was more important just now than his squeamish stomach.

It was night before Tom's request came to fruition. The deputy arrived to relieve the sheriff from his post. Tom heard the exchange of a few words, some whispered instructions, and then the sounds of the sheriff leaving and the deputy barring the door.

Tom was resting lazily on his bunk, thinking that perhaps the sheriff had decided to deny him the pipe, when the deputy appeared at the cell door holding a small package in his hands.

"Get up, Tom," commanded the deputy with authority. He was in charge with the sheriff gone, and he obviously expected the prisoner to do as he commanded.

"The town Selectmen in their generosity have agreed to present you with a pipe, a tin of flints, and a pouch of tobacco. They consider this to be your last request before hanging. 'Tis arranged that you'll be brought to Worcester tomorrow, and you surely will hang for your thievin' deeds."

Tom reached for the proffered items through the cell

bars. "Why, thank you, Deputy. How kind you be," Tom said in a sugared tone. He returned to his bunk and worked on packing and drawing his pipe to light while the deputy proceeded to fall asleep on a sheaf of papers stacked on the desk.

All through the night the deputy slept and snored, and all through the night Tom packed tobacco, lit, drew and puffed at the pipe. Although he felt nearly green with the sickening odor of burning tobacco and the acrid taste of smoke in his mouth, Tom worked with purpose and determination and overcame his revulsion.

As each pipeful of tobacco was smoked, the hot burned ashes were poured carefully onto the floor near the bunk. As the cold gray light of October dawn crept into the damp cell, Tom was ready.

"Deputy!" he called loudly. "Deputy!"

The deputy stirred from his uncomfortable hunched position on the hard desk top. He rubbed his neck stiffly and stretched his arms. Suddenly, he jumped to his feet and looked about the office, sniffing at the air.

Tom knew the odor of burning wood was strong, and the deputy feared that Tom had set the jail on fire in order to escape.

"What's wrong?" he demanded in confusion. "What's burning?"

Tom laughed a diabolical laugh that froze the deputy in his tracks, but his words were soft and smooth. "Burning?" he repeated. "I fear you've slept too soundly. All you smell is the smoke of my pipe. 'Tis merely the tobacco that smolders."

"Why did you call me?" the deputy asked, a quaver in his voice.

"I've called you to open this cell door," Tom said grimly. "I do not wish to remain here any longer."

"Are you teched?" the deputy responded with astonishment. "I can't let you out. Your life of theft has led you here, and you will stay until you go to Worcester to be hanged."

Tom's piercing blue eyes settled coldly on the deputy's, and Tom felt that his look was as powerful as a stranglehold. The deputy was too frightened to move. Tom stood stock still, his feet rooted to the floor.

" 'Tis said that I am in the service of the devil," he said in a deep, steady voice. "Some say I am the devil himself. Do you not believe it?"

The deputy swallowed hard, and Tom did not need, or wait for, an answer. "Where evil is, there am I," he continued, never wavering his fixed gaze. "I know your deepest sins and have writ your name upon my list, ready to drop your brown soul into my harvest basket to give to Beelzebub. Old Beelzebub is never satisfied. There are never enough souls for the keeper of Hell."

The deputy was sweating now, despite the chill in the air. He's probably reviewing all his sins and wondering if I could possibly know them all, Tom thought.

"How could you know my actions?" the deputy challenged with desperation. "It wouldn't be human!"

"Perhaps I am not human," Tom answered coldly. "Open the door and let me out or I'll have your foul soul this moment! If you do as I say, I'll not bother you again so long as you live."

Tom took a step forward from where he stood near the rumpled bunk. The deputy's eyes nearly burst from their sockets as he spied two smoldering cloven hooves etched in the floor, as though they had been burned in fire. Tom looked at the deputy and let out a shrieking laugh.

"Open the door and let me out!"

The deputy moved as if in a trance. Sweating and shaking, he thrust the key into the lock and stood aside as Tom strode out. The deputy never took his eyes off the cloven hooves burned in the floor, even as Tom unbarred the door and slammed it behind him.

XII · Home Preserves

Tom knew that news of his disappearance would be a hot
story, sure to spread through Westborough like a fire
through dry brush. Not wanting to miss the festivities and
also not wanting to be hanged after all his hard work, he
buried himself carefully in a huge stack of hay that sat near
the town stables, just opposite the jailhouse. Tom took a
nap in the soft hay, and by late morning he awoke to see a
large crowd gathered in front of the jail and growing so fast
that it soon extended all around his warm hiding place.

Townsfolk pushed and jostled at the cell window, some
balancing children on their shoulders, to see the chilling
sight of cloven hooves burned into the wooden floor. A
small group of men stood to one side of the haystack voicing
their support for banding together to recapture the prisoner
and hang him immediately.

Shouting voices reached his ears as the discussion was
joined by people of both persuasions. A passerby interrupted. "What's the fight?" he asked.

"Ain't you heard the news? 'Tis that bewitched Tom
Cook. When the deputy went to fetch him this morning, the
jail was locked up tight from the inside, but the cell was
empty, except for the mark of Beelzebub's hooves burnt
into the floor. You can see them for yourself. There's no
question he's the devil himself, for the devil can't be confined."

"You're right," Tom answered from behind the hay that
covered him.

A few people moved closer and a second man picked up

the conversation. "The fight here is, should we go after the cursed thief and hang him now, or do we let him be?"

"No mortal man can touch the devil!" argued a stout woman, pulling her shawl tighter about her shoulders. " 'Twill bring a curse on the whole town!"

"You're right!" Tom echoed.

"I say hang him and rid this town of his evil!" shouted another.

Through the stalks of hay that blocked his vision, Tom thought he saw Jesse work his way into the knot of people around him. When he heard the boy's voice, he was certain.

" 'Tis only Tom Cook you're talking about. He never hurt no one."

"Are you teched, boy? The man's bewitched. How do you think he escaped?"

The noise of the crowd grew louder as factions on both sides offered their arguments either for or against hanging. Then the door of the jailhouse opened and the sheriff stepped out with the shaken deputy beside him. He quieted the raucous group and began to speak. With their backs turned to the haystack, Tom arranged the sweet-smelling hay so that he had a clearer view.

"You all know Tom Cook is gone," the sheriff began. "We don't see no human way he could have got out, for the cell door is locked and the bars hold fast. It appears as though some supernatural power has removed the prisoner clean. There's no other explanation, and the sign of the cloven hooves is enough evidence for us."

The sheriff paused a moment and took a deep breath. "Now, there's some among you as think we ought to search for the thief straight off and hang him high."

"Aye! That we do!" yelled a voice in the crowd, and Tom

covered himself with the straw again. A small chorus of murmurs responded.

"And there's some as think this is the work of the devil and Tom had best be left alone," the sheriff continued.

"Let the devil be!" shouted the crowd in a wave of voices. "Let him be!"

"And so we shall," declared the sheriff. "We fit the laws of man and shall not mix with the work of the devil."

Reverend Parkman stepped up with the sheriff, and the crowd quieted. "There's no denying Beelzebub holds Tom Cook," he said. "I want no man to go against the sheriff's decision. 'Tis in God's hands now, and Tom Cook is to be left to himself from this day forward."

The crowd broke into a low murmur and began to disperse. Many were pleased, many disgruntled, but none would dispute the reverend's word.

Tom had harbored no doubts that the burned ashes from the pipe would leave their impression on the wooden floor and in the minds of the townsfolk for a long time to come. He had been equally certain that the deputy would not admit to letting Tom out of the cell. He was pleased that the tale of his disappearance was much improved since the deputy claimed he had simply vanished without a trace.

"He's safe," Tom heard Jesse breathe softly.

"You're right," Tom whispered back. Jesse glanced around him, looking at the faces of the few people who were left, trying to figure out who had agreed with him. Seeing no friendly faces, however, Tom saw the boy turn and walk jauntily toward home.

Tom was elated. He remained hidden until he was sure the crowd had gone. Then he crept unnoticed from the haystack. "This is certainly my most successful adventure yet," he congratulated himself as he threaded his way west through the cover of the trees and then turned south to cut through Wharton's fields.

Shortly Tom passed close to Wharton's farm, and as he did so, he spied five bushels of blackberries lined up on the back porch waiting for Cynthia to turn them into sweet preserves. Tom thought of all the time he had lost laying in his winter supplies on account of Wharton's stinginess, and it seemed fitting to him that the gentleman should contribute to his survival. *If I had not been in jail because of Wharton's complaint, I would have swelled my stores by now.* Without hesitation, he helped himself to one overflowing bushel and carted it home.

As Jesse peered cautiously through the window of Tom's cabin a short time later, he was surprised to see his friend casually stirring a pot of bubbling preserves over a blazing fire. He knocked at the window, and Tom looked up, to see his young friend pressing his nose flat against the thick pane. Tom laughed and waved the boy in. Jesse pulled the stool up to the fire while Tom continued his stirring.

"How'd you do it, Tom? The whole town's saying you just disappeared clean!"

Tom gave his friend a mysterious wink and said softly, "You're right." The boy glared at him incredulously, but Tom did not give him a chance to question him further. "Let's just say that folks are too eager to believe a tale, Jess. Things aren't always what they seem, you know."

Jesse regarded Tom with open admiration. "I want to be just like you when I grow up. Will you teach me everything you know?"

"There's no one who can be just like Tom Cook, for there's none other who carries the burden of the devil's ways as I must. 'Tis true I have enjoyed many an adventure, but there's been countless times that I would have traded my lot for the calm of working a farm and caring for a family.''

The tone of wistfulness that had crept into Tom's voice was quickly dispelled. '' 'Course, that doesn't mean I'm not happy, mind you. 'Tis a fine life for me, but as for Jesse Baxter, he's got to join the Meeting and learn to help folks in the ways of the town. You can do much more with the voice of authority.''

Tom ladled preserves carefully into glass jars and sealed each one with a layer of melted wax. Jesse pondered Tom's advice, and the pair shared a long moment of silence.

"Say," Tom said suddenly. "What are you doing hangin' about in the middle of the day?'' He gave Jesse a playful swat. "Get your club-tail out of here and head for school!''

Jesse grinned sheepishly and headed for the door. "I guess the sheriff's too spooked to come after you again. At least you're safe. Can I come by in the morning before school?''

Tom laughed. "I'm safe, all right. After this adventure, I doubt there's a living creature in all of Westborough who'll venture to cross the Leveller! See you tomorrow, Jesse.''

Tom was filled with energy, and after setting his preserves carefully aside, he spent the remainder of the day laying in whatever food was still to be gathered from the forest. A few soft apples still clung to the trees near the Stones' house, and Tom helped himself to an armload after nonchalantly returning the empty bushel basket to Wharton's back porch.

Dried apples, nuts, berries, and wild roots went into Tom's store of food. He laid out his traps and thought ahead to the strong smell of rabbit stew. After a full day, Tom let the fire die down in the grate, hung his suspenders on their accustomed hook, laid his shirt on the chair, and wearily crawled into bed. He left his britches on, though, just in case the sheriff changed his mind.

There was so much to be done, now that his neck was saved, and Tom looked forward to the busy days ahead. Even, he thought tiredly, to the quiet coziness of a snowed-in winter.

XIII · The Devil's Due

TOM SLEPT SOUNDLY that night, comfortable in his familiar bed and free from the worry of hanging. The day dawned gray and drizzly, and without the sun to rouse him, Tom slept later than usual. He never heard the sound of footsteps on his cabin floor or saw the fire leap into flame, but through his dreams he heard his name called deep and low and he opened his eyes with a start.

"Arise, Thomas Cook. Arise and come with me. 'Tis time for you to enter upon another life."

Tom jumped from the bed and saw the old man from the forest clearing standing in front of the hearth. Tom's blood froze in his body and fear choked his voice. The Wicked One was dressed in his long black cloak, his wizened face nearly covered by the hood, and his bony finger pointed at Tom accusingly as he walked forward slowly until he was but a few feet from Tom. The younger man could feel the devil's breath hot against his cheeks.

" 'Tis time for me to collect what is due, Thomas Cook. You have done nothing to become a part of the bargain that was struck so many years ago. For all your petty thievings and your mischievous ways, you do not mark my bidding. I am done with you. 'Tis time for you to come with me."

The wrinkled old man turned his back on Tom and walked closer to the fire, which glowed and grew as he approached, sending flames leaping up the chimney flue. He bent down slowly and picked up a wicker basket in one hand. He moved as if weary, out of habit more than determination. With his free hand, he menacingly opened the lid.

"No!" begged Tom desperately. "Not now. I'm not ready. Not ready! I need more time."

"No one is ever ready for time to run out, Thomas Cook," countered Beelzebub, and it seemed to Tom that a note of satisfaction had crept into the old man's voice.

Tom stood before the Wicked One, his britches hanging low and his long johns showing above. The devil would show no mercy, and his voice grew hard. "I will close your mother's bargain now."

Shivers of fear tingled along Tom's spine, and sweat beaded on his forehead. He knew he had to outwit the devil, but he could not think clearly. Despite his vow, made the night of his encounter with Beelzebub in the clearing, the Wicked One had again caught him unprepared.

I need more time, he thought desperately. I must hold him off. He raised his face toward the devil's wizened one and questioned him. "Why would you want a Bible-toting man such as myself? I live a humble and charitable life. I am tempted by naught and give away all that I come by. 'Tis a godly man I be, helping others at every turn."

The devil let out a mocking laugh. "You fancy yourself a godly man, do you? So do many who dwell in my abode even now. So many humble and Godfearing souls! You're a common thief, Thomas Cook, and your sins alone condemn you!"

"Not a thief, Beelzebub, a leveller. I give away all that I take to those who are in need. I never yield to temptation."

"So many strong words for such a weak man, Thomas. Were you never tempted by Goody Stone's comforter? Remember the warmth of that comforter, Thomas, so plump and downy? You wanted it for your own, did you not?"

" 'Twas your temptation that led me astray," Tom complained. "You blew the wind so cold about me." Then Tom took the advantage in the argument. "I gave it to the Baxters all the same, did I not? I did not yield even then."

Beelzebub was not about to back down. "What about the pudding you stole from James Wharton's pot? You would have ripped it open and devoured the whole thing. You did not give a thought to charity then!"

Tom remembered the hot, meaty pudding that he had so carefully lifted from Wharton's kitchen-room. He might have yielded to hunger if he had been left undisturbed.

"Your trickery again, old man," Tom said accusingly. "You thought to trip me up and tease my mind till I was near sick with hunger and the smell of that tantalizin' pudding. I survived your calling partridges, your pungent spices, and your call of gluttony. I worked hard to deliver that pudding to the Ludlows and treat them with honor, to boot. I touched not a morsel of that feast!"

Beelzebub threw the cloak from about his head, and Tom began to sweat as the fire, unfueled by any log, heated the room warmer than it had ever been. Beelzebub clutched his basket tighter upon his arm and glowered at Tom.

"I'll not play games with you and lose, Thomas Cook. Your sins are many. Do you not recall the fish you stole from James Wharton? You have plagued the man!"

"The perch went to feed the apple pickers at Baxter's cider pressing," Tom protested. "I helped with the work and paid for my trouble with my fingers!"

"Your help was worth nothing!" Beelzebub bellowed. "You jammed the press and fouled the day's work in a trice. And what about Wharton's wig? 'Twas thievery and meanness to my seasoned eyes."

"The wig was just a joke," Tom pleaded. He was sweating heavily now, feeling that he was losing the battle with Beelzebub. " 'Twas a joke and trick for all Wharton's snobbery. I meant nothin' by it."

Beelzebub leaned his face closer to Tom's and fingered the lid on his basket. "You never let Wharton alone, do you? You torment him. Think on the flour you stole from his wagon, trotting about the countryside delivering his supplies to every soul about. And what about the blackberries? You kept those for yourself, did you not?"

I'm lost, Tom thought fearfully. I cannot make an answer for my every act. A man has got to live. God help me!

Just then a slight movement outside the cabin window caught Tom's eye. Stealthily, he focused his eyes at the glass and saw Jesse's ashen face peering at the scene inside. The boy's hand was stopped in midair, as if he had been just about to knock.

'Tis the boy, Tom thought in alarm. He can't see me lost in Beelzebub's basket. I've got to outwit the devil or all is lost. 'Tis worth more than just my soul, now.

Beelzebub was intent on his verbal battle with Tom and was unaware that Jesse had come to the window and that Tom's mind was focused with renewed energy on winning his battle.

He pulled a yellowed paper from under his cloak. "I gave you all your life, Thomas Cook, and exchanged that for your soul. Here is the pact that makes you mine, signed by your own mother."

Tom listened with trembling breath to Beelzebub's words, but his thoughts concentrated on Jesse. The sight of the youth had sparked a fleeting recollection of the many times they had shared in the cabin, and the sight of his obvious terror startled Tom into alertness. He remembered how Jesse had teased him about the old suspenders and how Tom had joked that it would take the devil himself to make him part with the worn galluses.

Suddenly Tom was sobered and his mind sharp. That was the very bargain he would strike with the Wicked One—he would trade his suspenders to save his soul. Of course, his tormentor would not agree willingly to such a deal. I will have to outwit him, Tom thought, and I know just how to do it.

The Leveller raised his eyes to Beelzebub's, but the devil was gloating now, sure he had claimed Tom's soul for eternity, and he did not see the strength and confidence in his opponent's gaze. He waved the yellowed parchment pact in Tom's face and declared firmly, " 'Tis signed plainly, Eunice Forbush Cook."

Tom's face was pale, and it distracted the devil from looking at the blue eyes that sparkled with anticipation. He continued, "Had you chosen to follow my ways and do my bidding, I would have spared you more time on earth and given you all the worldly pleasures, but you thwart me at every turn. I'll take your soul and all your petty sins now and you shall do my bidding in Hell!"

Tom lowered his eyes in mock penitence and fear. "You have my soul in your keeping, Beelzebub. I am lost." Tom raised his eyes fearfully from the floor. He hiked up his drooping britches and then asked plaintively, "Will you just wait until I draw my suspenders on?"

"Aye," the Wicked One said condescendingly. "I'll wait for that."

Tom reached for his suspenders from the hook near the fireplace, and Beelzebub opened his basket expectantly. Slowly calculating every movement, Tom buttoned on his suspenders, letting them hang down against his legs. With a thumb under each strap, he pulled the suspenders up toward his shoulders.

"I said I'd not take you till you draw on your galluses," Beelzebub broke in, "but I'll not wait forever."

"Aye, but you will!" Tom shouted. He yanked the suspenders from his pants, their buttons flying, and with his gnarled hand, he gathered them into a ball and threw them quickly into the blazing fire. As they writhed and melted into ashes, Tom leaped high in the air and with a victorious laugh, shook his fist at his tormentor.

"You've made your promise now. You can never touch my soul till I put on my suspenders. The pair you see melted in the fire is the last pair I'll ever own. I swear before God I'll never draw on another pair!"

The realization of Tom's trickery dawned slowly on Beelzebub. He had agreed to wait until Tom put on his suspenders before he would take his soul, and now his chance was gone. When he discovered how he had been outwitted, his face turned white with rage. He cursed and swore and thrashed his arms about, the basket swinging wildly from his arm. Still, Tom stood his ground, his hands set mockingly on his hips and his pants hanging low.

The devil pointed his bony finger at Tom and spoke in a low and menacing voice. "I'll bide my time and follow close until that moment when you once forget. Then I shall be there to collect what you owe!"

With those parting words, the devil vanished, cloak and all, and not a trace was left, not even the shape of his cloven hooves. Tom let out a yelp and a holler and ran for the door. He surrounded Jesse with a crushing embrace and hugged the boy with all his might.

Finally, Jesse believed what his eyes had seen, and the two danced merrily into the cabin, whooping and hollering and slapping each other on the back.

"You've surely come in puddin' time, Jesse. You've saved me, sure as God. When I saw your frightened face at the window, it put me in mind of all the happy times we shared, and how you teased me so often about them worn-out galluses. I told you 'twould take the devil himself to make me give them up, and when I recollected that, I knew what I'd do to outwit him once and for all.''

"You're saved!" Jesse crowed. "And you're safe as long as you mind your promise and never put on another pair of suspenders.'' He paused for a minute and then burst out in an uncontrollable laugh. "How will you hold up your sagging pants? Your drawers will droop!'' he chortled. "You'll have to eat till your belly holds them up!''

"Who cares a fig for droopin' drawers, Jess? Why, I'd wear your mother's apron if it would save my soul!''

The tale of Tom's encounter with the devil was soon on the tip of every wagging tongue, and the Leveller's life was considerably easier after that. Many of the families in town paid regular visits to Tom's cabin, depositing a tithe of their bounty and knowing that Tom would redistribute it to those who were most in need. Those who claimed they did not believe he had outwitted the Wicked One began to think of him as an eccentric, "a little teched,'' and left him to himself.

And as for Tom, he was never seen to hold up his pants with anything but a simple rope, looped about his waist and tied in front with a neat square knot.

Afterword

THOMAS COOK WAS born on October 6, 1738, in the village of Westborough, Massachusetts, the son of blacksmith Cornelius Cook and his wife, Eunice. The unusual gray plaster house in which he first opened his eyes to the world still stands on the corner of East Main and Lyman Streets in the center of the still small town, set back from the road and partially hidden by massive ancient oaks.

As one of ten children in the Cook family, Tom received little attention until, at the age of three, he miraculously recovered from what was judged to be a fatal fever. Rumors flew throughout the village folk that Tom's mother had pledged her son's soul to the devil in return for his recovery. The story took a firm hold among the superstitious and religious people, and from that time forward, Tom was shunned by all around him. His every success was seen as the devil's work, and as he grew older, his entire family suffered from his ostracism. At the early age of 14, his family moved from town to try to gain a more prosperous livelihood, and Tom was left to fend for himself.

The boy became adept at settling into abandoned cabins and storage houses and learned to use his wits to survive. History records that he came to be both loved and feared by his New England neighbors, for he developed the knack of levelling off the fortunes of the farmers about, appropriating the bounty of those who enjoyed plentiful harvests for those who barely managed to survive. While many prosperous farmers called him a thief, Tom called himself a leveller.

Many legends concerning Tom's escapades are recorded in the town's archives, and an unexplained meeting with the

Reverend Ebenezer Parkman was duly noted in the venerable man's extensive diary. Yet no explanation of how Tom accomplished his feats is offered, except to note that Tom knew the daily routine of all the families in town.

A few of the tales have been adapted and incorporated into this book, and others have been invented to conform with the types of adventures Tom undertook. He managed to keep most of his exploits secret, but when caught, he learned how to manipulate others' fear that he was bewitched to avoid punishment.

Tom did not have any trouble with Beelzebub from the moment he threw his suspenders into the fire. He survived the winter of 1779–80, when a fierce January blizzard covered entire cabins to the roof, and he lived through many more hard New England winters that followed. In fact, although he suffered several accidents that left him less and less agile, Tom lived through the rest of the century and made a good dent into the next one as well.

He marked the death of the Reverend Mr. Parkman, saw his country stand shakily on its feet, watched shillings and pounds become dimes and dollars, and saw the once-rare stage line become a daily run through Westborough, carrying travelers from Worcester to Boston.

Tom kept up his travels and adventures for as long as his health would allow, but old age and failing agility finally placed a heavy hand on him. As with many of the elderly residents of Westborough, Tom finally had to "come on the town," moving down Upton Road to the Levi Bowman farm, where the town grudgingly boarded its poor. There he stayed until the proud age of eighty-nine, when an apparent spark of wanderlust led him back to the familiar roads and meadows that he had once known. In 1827, along the Bay Path to Boston, the Final Leveller overtook Tom Cook.

In his death, he unwittingly played one final joke on the

tested patience of the town, for it is recorded that the Selectmen of Westborough met and voted to expend the sum of forty dollars to have the body of Thomas Cook returned to the town and given proper burial.

Those who knew the story of Thomas Cook and the devil would stop each other on the street to share the news of the Leveller's death, but as to whether Tom had died with his suspenders on or off, there were none who would say. Whenever someone chanced to ask, those who knew would simply give their questioner a knowing wink, a mysterious smile, and a standard answer: "What do you think?"